'Don't!' Lexie gasped, stepping back as she saw Lucan's intent in the raw hunger of his dark gaze.

'This is *so* not a good idea, Lucan!' She put her hands up to stop him as he followed her, those hands becoming crushed between them as Lucan leaned his body into hers so that they were now touching from breast to thigh.

'It feels like a very good idea to me,' Lucan assured her softly as his arms moved either side of her, so that his hands could grip the worktop behind her, effectively trapping her between his arms as the heat of his body fitted against her much softer curves. 'Doesn't it feel like a good idea to you, Lexie?' he prompted huskily.

Council

D0774674

THE SCANDALOUS ST CLAIRES

Three arrogant aristocrats—ready to marry!

Don't miss any of Carole Mortimer's
fabulous trilogy:

January—
JORDAN ST CLAIRE:
DARK AND DANGEROUS

February—
LUCAN ST CLAIRE

March—
GIDEON ST CLAIRE

And read where it all began—
with *The Notorious St Claires,* in Regency
England!

Only in Mills & Boon® Historical Romance,
out this month
LADY ARABELLA'S SCANDALOUS MARRIAGE

THE RELUCTANT DUKE

BY
CAROLE MORTIMER

MILLS & BOON

To Pete

DID YOU PURCHASE THIS BOOK WITHOUT A COVER?

If you did, you should be aware it is **stolen property** as it was reported *unsold and destroyed* by a retailer. Neither the author nor the publisher has received any payment for this book.

All the characters in this book have no existence outside the imagination of the author, and have no relation whatsoever to anyone bearing the same name or names. They are not even distantly inspired by any individual known or unknown to the author, and all the incidents are pure invention.

All Rights Reserved including the right of reproduction in whole or in part in any form. This edition is published by arrangement with Harlequin Enterprises II BV/S.à.r.l. The text of this publication or any part thereof may not be reproduced or transmitted in any form or by any means, electronic or mechanical, including photocopying, recording, storage in an information retrieval system, or otherwise, without the written permission of the publisher.

This book is sold subject to the condition that it shall not, by way of trade or otherwise, be lent, resold, hired out or otherwise circulated without the prior consent of the publisher in any form of binding or cover other than that in which it is published and without a similar condition including this condition being imposed on the subsequent purchaser.

® and TM are trademarks owned and used by the trademark owner and/or its licensee. Trademarks marked with ® are registered with the United Kingdom Patent Office and/or the Office for Harmonisation in the Internal Market and in other countries.

First published in Great Britain 2011
Harlequin Mills & Boon Limited,
Eton House, 18-24 Paradise Road, Richmond, Surrey TW9 1SR

© Carole Mortimer 2011

ISBN: 978 0 263 88629 0

Harlequin Mills & Boon policy is to use papers that are natural, renewable and recyclable products and made from wood grown in sustainable forests. The logging and manufacturing process conform to the legal environmental regulations of the country of origin.

Printed and bound in Spain
by Litografia Rosés, S.A., Barcelona

THE RELUCTANT DUKE

Carole Mortimer was born in England, the youngest of three children. She began writing in 1978, and has now written over one hundred and fifty books for Harlequin Mills & Boon. Carole has six sons: Matthew, Joshua, Timothy, Michael, David and Peter. She says, 'I'm happily married to Peter senior; we're best friends as well as lovers, which is probably the best recipe for a successful relationship. We live in a lovely part of England.'

CHAPTER ONE

'HAPPY New Year, Mr St Claire!'

Lucan—the Mr St Claire referred to—stood frowning in front of the huge picture window in his executive office on the tenth floor of the St Claire Corporation building.

It was still early on this cold and frosty January morning, only eight-thirty, but Lucan had been at his desk working since six o'clock, in order to deal with some of the work needing his attention following the long Christmas and New Year break.

At least he had *told* himself he needed to come in early in order to deal with the work needing his attention. The truth was he had been only too glad to get back to normality after he and his two younger brothers had spent a traditional Christmas at his mother's home in Edinburgh, before all of them had decamped briefly—but not briefly enough for Lucan!—to Mulberry Hall, the family estate in Gloucestershire, to attend his youngest brother's wedding there on New Year's Eve.

Lucan had understood Jordan and Stephanie's reasons for wanting the wedding to be held there—it was where the two of them had met, after all—but as soon as he'd been able to do so politely, Lucan had made his excuses and gone to Klosters, skiing for three days.

He turned now, that frown still creasing his brow as he

looked at the young woman who had just stepped in from the office that adjoined his. The office belonging to his PA. Except the woman standing in the doorway *wasn't* his PA. Wasn't anyone Lucan had ever set eyes on before, in fact!

She was probably aged in her mid-twenties, very slender and a couple of inches over five feet tall. The black business suit and the snowy white blouse she wore beneath it took absolutely nothing away from the gypsy-wild effect of her long ebony hair as it cascaded riotously over her shoulders and down her back. Equally black brows were raised over eyes of a deep sparkling blue, surrounded by thick sooty lashes, and a small straight nose above sinfully and sensually full lips.

Lips that immediately—surprisingly!—stirred Lucan's body into arousal as his thoughts shifted smoothly to bedrooms, and hot and nakedly entwined bodies. Surprisingly because it was widely acknowledged that successful businessman Lucan St Claire was as ruthless emotionally in the brief relationships he had with women as he was in the boardroom.

Lucan didn't feel in the least ruthless as he stared at this dark and untamed beauty!

He scowled darkly. 'Who the hell are you?'

Lexie might almost have felt sorry for Lucan St Claire's expression of scowling bewilderment if it hadn't been for the fact that he had so obviously brought this present situation completely upon himself.

If he weren't so coldly self-absorbed, so arrogantly unable to relate to the people who worked for and with him, then perhaps his PA wouldn't have decided to walk out on him on Christmas Eve, without even bothering to tell him she was going.

Perhaps.

Lexie had a suspicion that Jessica Brown's interest in Lucan St Claire hadn't all been business-related, and that his lack of interest in return—or inability to feel any—had been the reason the other woman had finally left so abruptly…

Lexie walked over to stand in front of the imposing oak desk, aware of the ease of power that surrounded Lucan St Claire as he towered on the other side of that desk. Aware of how comfortably he wore the charcoal-grey tailored suit, and the pale grey silk shirt with a darker grey tie knotted meticulously at his throat.

This man wasn't only tall and impeccably dressed, but aristocratically handsome, too, Lexie allowed grudgingly. Although, in her opinion the dark, almost black, hair could have been worn a little longer than it was, and those powerful good looks—enigmatic black eyes, haughtily long nose, chiselled lips above a square-cut and determined chin—were stamped with a haughty arrogance she didn't find in the least appealing.

Not that there had ever been any likelihood of Lexie finding *anything* appealing about a single member of the St Claire family! Her mouth twisted derisively.

'My name is Lexie Hamilton, Mr St Claire. I'm your temporary temporary PA,' she said as he still scowled.

Those dark eyes narrowed chillingly. 'It's news to me that I'm in need of a temporary PA, let alone a temporary *temporary* one…'

Lexie's derision deepened. 'Your ex-PA called my agency on Christmas Eve to arrange for a temporary replacement until you are in a position to arrange for a permanent one. Unfortunately, the lady most qualified for the position isn't available for another three days.'

Lucan St Claire looked totally baffled by this explanation—as well he might.

Lexie had decided before coming here that even the curiosity she had always felt concerning the St Claire family should have its time limit. Three days would be quite long enough for her to confirm every bad thing she had ever thought or heard of them.

As it turned out, she had overestimated—three *minutes* in this cold and haughty man's company was quite long enough for her to know he believed himself to be arrogantly superior!

His scowl deepened. 'Exactly why and when did Jennifer make these arrangements?'

Now it was Lexie's turn to frown. 'I thought your PA's name was Jessica…?'

'Jennifer—Jessica,' Lucan St Claire dismissed irritably. 'Her name is of little relevance if, as you say, she has now left my employment.'

Lexie gave a rueful smile. 'Perhaps if you had taken the trouble to remember her name she wouldn't have felt the need to leave so abruptly…?'

Lucan's eyes narrowed to steely slits. 'When I want your opinion, Miss Hamilton, then you can be assured I will ask for it!'

'I was merely pointing out—'

'Something that I believe, as a *temporary* temporary employee, is absolutely none of your business?' Lucan rasped harshly.

'Probably not,' she conceded with a rueful grimace.

An attitude completely lacking in genuine apology, Lucan recognised with a dark frown. 'Why would Jen—Jessica,' he corrected irritably, 'leave in that unprofessional way?'

Lexie Hamilton gave a shrug. 'I believe she mentioned

to someone at the agency that the final insult came when you didn't even bother to send her so much as a Christmas card—let alone buy her a present.'

'She received a Christmas bonus in her pay cheque last month—the same as all my other employees.'

'A *personal* Christmas present,' Lexie Hamilton drawled pointedly.

'Why on earth would I do that?' Lucan was genuinely astounded by the accusation.

'I believe it's customary for one's immediate boss to— never mind,' the raven-haired beauty dismissed, as she obviously saw his impatience. 'I had no idea you were already in your office—I took a call just now that I believe is in need of your immediate attention. I wrote the details down for you.' She handed him a slip of paper.

Lucan glanced down at the neatly written message before crushing it in his hand.

John Barton, the caretaker of Mulberry Hall, was reporting some damage to the west gallery of the house, following the rapid thaw over the last two days. Damage that John believed was in need of Lucan's personal attention.

As the eldest of the three St Claire brothers, Lucan had inherited the Mulberry Hall estate on the death of their father eight years ago. But it was an estate he had rarely visited following his parents' separation and acrimonious divorce twenty-five years ago, and a place he certainly had no inclination to return to again so soon after his last visit.

The first eleven of Lucan's thirty-six years had been spent happily living at Mulberry Hall with both his parents. The three brothers had been in complete ignorance of their father's affair with a widow who lived in one of the cottages on the estate with her grown-up daughter. Or of the unhappiness that affair had caused their mother. An unhappiness that had imploded twenty-five years ago and resulted in Molly moving back to Scotland and taking her three sons with her.

Lucan had forced himself to return to Mulberry Hall for Jordan and Stephanie's wedding, almost a week ago, as no doubt had his brother Gideon, and their mother; to be asked to go back there again so soon was unacceptable.

Barton had said the damage was in the west gallery…

That was the long picture gallery, where the portrait of Lucan's father, Alexander St Claire, the previous Duke of Stourbridge, now hung in majestic state.

A portrait which revealed that Lucan, of all the three St Claire brothers, most resembled their dark-haired, dark-eyed and adulterous father!

'Mr Barton sounded as if he considered the matter urgent,' Lexie Hamilton told him now, and she looked pointedly at the message she had written out so neatly, which Lucan had crushed in his hand.

'I believe that is for me to decide, don't you?' His voice was silky soft.

'It's probably too late for me to do anything about your ten o'clock appointment.' She completely ignored his set-down. 'But I could probably cancel the rest of your appointments for the next couple of days if you were thinking of—'

'Believe me, Miss Hamilton, you really don't want to know what I'm thinking right now,' Lucan assured her harshly. 'My priority at the moment is to speak to the person in charge at your agency.'

'Why?'

Lucan raised his brows. 'I'm not accustomed to having my actions questioned.'

Lexie easily picked up on the unspoken words—least of all by a temporary, temporary employee. But the person in charge at the agency at the moment happened to be Lexie herself, since her parents, the owners of Premier Personnel, had embarked on a three-week cruise the day after Christmas, in celebration of their twenty-fifth wedding anniversary.

Her parents weren't even aware of the call that had come into the agency from Lucan St Claire's PA on Christmas Eve.

Lexie had told herself at the time that she hadn't told them because she didn't want to put any sort of cloud over her parents' excitement by so much as *mentioning* the St Claire family.

She had *told* herself that was the reason...

Initially Lexie had been so stunned by the identity of the caller that she had just taken down the details, before woodenly assuring Jessica Brown that she was not to worry, that Premier Personnel would take care of the problem.

It was only after the call had ended that Lexie had realised the possibilities that call had just opened up for her.

She was qualified for the job—just—and it was always quiet in the offices of Premier Personnel in January. Three days. Just three days, she had promised herself. Spent observing Lucan St Claire, the reputedly powerful and ruthless owner of the St Claire Corporation.

So far Lucan St Claire was proving to be everything Lexie had ever imagined he might be!

She straightened to her full height of five feet and three inches in her two-inch-high shoes. 'I assure you that I am qualified to stand in here for three days, Mr St Claire.'

Those dark eyes viewed her coldly. 'I don't believe I questioned your qualifications...'

Lexie felt irritated colour warm her cheeks. 'Nonetheless, the implication was there.'

'Really?' Lucan drawled as he moved to lean against

the side of his desk, bringing himself down onto a level with Lexie Hamilton's indignant blue eyes, and enabling him to see the perfection of her creamy skin, and the small and determined chin beneath those highly sensual—sexual—lips…

Lips like that—so moist and full, so softly pouting—could drive a man wild when applied to a certain part of his anatomy—

Lucan abruptly moved away, dismayed at the inappropriate imaginings he was having about this less-than-polite young woman, and full of self-disgust at the hardening of that certain part of his own anatomy!

'What's the name of your agency?' he bit out harshly.

'Premier Personnel,' Lexie Hamilton supplied with a frown. 'But wouldn't you like me to put through a call to Mr Barton first? He implied the matter was of some urgency—'

'I believe I'm perfectly capable of prioritising my own workload, Lexie,' Lucan rasped dismissively.

'Of course.' She nodded abruptly, a frown still between those deep blue eyes as she turned and hurried across the room, giving Lucan an unobstructed view of that long and riotous ebony-coloured hair. He could also view the provocative sway of her shapely bottom underneath the short black skirt and above slender and shapely legs.

Telling Lucan that this young woman was *just* as qualified to share his bed as she was to be his temporary, temporary PA!

'Did Jemima change the colour of her hair?'

Lucan turned slowly to look at his brother Gideon, where he stood silhouetted in the doorway leading out to the hallway. The younger man was frowning across at the closed door between the two offices with the same perplexed expression Lucan was sure had been on his own face fifteen minutes ago, when Lexie Hamilton had first made her entrance.

It gave Lucan some satisfaction to realise that Gideon had also got his PA's name wrong. His *ex*-PA, Lucan corrected irritably.

It was unbelievable that Jen—Jessica should have just walked out on him without so much as giving notice. It was even more irritating that her temporary temporary replacement should be the beautiful and totally distracting Lexie Hamilton.

Lucan gave an impatient shake of his head as he moved back behind his desk and sat down. 'Her name was Jessica.' Apparently! 'And that wasn't her,' he added stonily.

'No?' Gideon murmured with a frown as he strolled farther into the room. At thirty-four, two years Lucan's junior, Gideon was tall and blond, with piercing dark eyes set in a strikingly handsome face. 'I didn't realise you were going to replace her.'

'I wasn't,' Lucan bit out tightly, as he recalled the reasons Lexie had given him for Jessica Brown having walked out on him in that totally unprofessional way.

He somehow doubted that Lexie would ever allow her own presence to be overlooked in the same way—even for the three days she had said she intended working for him...

'No?' Gideon raised surprised brows. 'Then who was *that*?'

'A temp,' Lucan dismissed impatiently. A *temporary* temp!

'Oh.' Gideon nodded. 'She looks vaguely familiar...'

Lucan's interest sharpened. 'In what way?'

'I have no idea.' His brother gave a self-derisive grimace. 'It's a sad state of affairs, Lucan, when all the beautiful women you meet start to look alike!'

As far as Lucan was concerned Lexie didn't look or behave like any other woman he had ever met! Something he found intriguing in spite of himself.

'What can I do for you, Gideon?' He deliberately changed the subject, having no intention of discussing Lexie any further with his brother. Or of allowing Gideon to realise his instant and totally unprecedented physical response to her unusual gypsy-wild beauty.

Lucan always dated models and actresses—although 'dated' was perhaps a slight exaggeration! What he usually did was take models and actresses out to dinner, or, in the case of the latter, escort them to film premieres, and then invariably to his bed. Beautiful women, perfectly groomed and sophisticated women—women who didn't expect any serious involvement with him and were just happy to be seen with the rich and powerful Lucan St Claire.

He had certainly never been in the least interested in becoming involved with one of his employees—as proved by the fact that he hadn't even got the name of his last PA right—and it probably wouldn't be a good idea to make Lexie Hamilton the exception to that rule, either!

Gideon raised surprised blond brows. 'Don't tell me you've forgotten that you asked me to come in at nine o'clock this morning, so that we could go over the contracts together before Andrew Proctor arrives at ten?'

As the legal representative for all the St Claire Corporation's dealings, Gideon kept an office just down the hallway from this one, as well as having his own private offices in the city.

Lucan *had* forgotten Gideon was coming in this morning—a phenomenon completely unheard of until today; business had always come first, second and last with Lucan.

Gideon gave a speculative smile. 'Miss Whatever-her-name-is should sit in on the meeting—Proctor will be so distracted by the way she looks he won't have any idea what he's signing!'

'Her name is Lexie Hamilton,' Lucan supplied harshly. 'And I would prefer Andrew Proctor to know *exactly* what he's signing. I also don't think it appropriate for you to make such personal remarks about an employee, Gideon,' he added darkly.

'I didn't arrive soon enough to actually see her face, but any man with red blood still flowing in his veins couldn't help but notice that pert little bottom!' his brother assured him dryly.

A frown creased Lucan's brow as he realised he wasn't altogether sure he felt comfortable discussing his outspoken but definitely sexy temporary temp in these terms—even with Gideon. 'Perhaps she might prove too much of a distraction?'

His brother raised mocking brows. 'Too much of a distraction…?'

Once again Lucan stood up restlessly. 'Not to me personally, of course,' he bit out tersely.

'No?'

Lucan felt his irritation deepen. 'No!'

'Then there's no problem with her sitting in on the meeting later this morning, is there?' Gideon dismissed practically.

No problem at all—except that Lucan already *knew* Lexie was likely to prove as much of a distraction to him as she was to anyone else!

'I had a call from John Barton this morning, concerning some damage to Mulberry Hall that needs looking at.' Lucan firmly changed the subject. 'I don't suppose you feel like going back to Gloucestershire for a few days…?'

'I don't suppose I do,' his brother came back firmly.

Exactly what Lucan had thought Gideon might say…

* * *

Lexie was fully aware of Lucan St Claire's presence as he came through from the adjoining office fifteen minutes later, to stand looking down at her broodingly from the other side of her desk. She was so aware of him that she deliberately ignored him as she kept typing into her laptop, until she had finished writing an email to Brenda, in the office at Premier Personnel, after the other woman had emailed Lexie to tell her she had successfully managed to reassure Lucan St Claire that Lexie Hamilton was indeed a temp sent from their agency.

Lexie had panicked slightly when Lucan St Claire had told her he intended telephoning Premier Personnel himself. She'd hurried back into the adjoining office to quickly put a call through to Brenda, her assistant in her parents' absence, to explain, and also arrange to meet Brenda for coffee after work this evening, so that she could explain the situation more fully.

Although Lexie wasn't one hundred per cent certain she could completely explain this situation to *herself*, let alone a third party.

It had been pure impulse—along with a lot of curiosity!—that had prompted her into coming here in the first place. An impulse and a curiosity she already regretted…

She hadn't expected to like the powerful Lucan St Claire, and she didn't. She had already decided after their brief conversation earlier that his reputation for being cold and arrogant was well justified. But there was no denying that he was strikingly handsome, too…

His colouring—that dark hair and those piercing jet-black eyes, his sculptured features—reminded Lexie so much of his father, Alexander…

She looked up at him blandly. 'Is there a problem with the intercom, Mr St Claire…?'

Lucan's mouth thinned at her obvious sarcasm. 'I accept that we got off to something of a bad start earlier, Miss Hamilton, but let's get one thing clear, shall we?' He looked down at her coldly. 'Namely, for the moment, *I* am the employer and *you* are the employee!'

Dark brows rose over those deep, and perhaps deliberately innocent, blue eyes. 'I am?'

'For the moment, yes,' he repeated harshly—warningly.

Lexie shrugged. 'Can I take it from that remark that Premier Personnel have confirmed that my replacement will arrive in three days' time?'

'You can,' Lucan confirmed tightly. 'It would appear that we are stuck with each other until then.'

She smiled slightly. 'My sentiments exactly.'

Lucan scowled darkly. 'Tell me, Lexie, is this tendency you have to be less than respectful to your employers also the reason that you find it easier to work for an agency rather than attempting to find a permanent position?'

Two bright spots of angry colour had appeared in the delicate cream of her cheeks. 'I don't believe my reasons to be any of your concern, Mr St Claire!'

He shrugged broad and muscled shoulders beneath his tailored jacket. 'I was curious. Nothing more,' he dismissed coolly.

As Lexie had long been curious about all of the St Claire family...

'I assure you, Mr St Claire, there is nothing about my personal life that would be of the least interest to you.' She looked up at him challengingly.

He raised dark brows. 'You sound very certain of that.'

'I am,' she came back evenly.

What would this man do or say, Lexie wondered, if he

were to learn that her grandmother was none other than Sian Thomas—the widow that his own father, Alexander St Claire, had fallen in love with over twenty-five years ago? The same woman all the St Claire family had treated with such contempt for those same many years… If he were to realise that Lexie's own full name, Alexandra, had been chosen in honour of 'Grandpa Alex', as she had called *this* man's father for the first sixteen of her twenty-four years…!

CHAPTER TWO

LEXIE had been in complete ignorance for most of her childhood as to exactly who her Grandpa Alex was—apart from being her step-grandfather, of course—but once she'd reached her teens her mother had quietly and calmly sat her down and explained the situation to her.

It was then that Lexie had learned that Alexander St Claire was actually the Duke of Stourbridge, and had been virtually disowned by his three sons after his divorce from their mother, Molly St Claire.

Lexie had instantly decided that all three of the St Claire brothers had treated their father abominably—simply because he had fallen in love with her gentle and beautiful grandmother. A woman none of the brothers had even attempted to meet, let alone get to know. If they had then they might have realised how far removed Sian was from being the *femme fatale* they so obviously believed her to be. They would also have seen how much she had loved their father. How much their father had loved her in return.

As it was, despite the fact that their father was now her Grandpa Alex, Lexie hadn't so much as set eyes on any of the three St Claire brothers until Alexander had died eight years ago, when they had dutifully arranged and attended their father's funeral at the village church in Stourbridge.

Lexie had attended the funeral, too, out of sheer bloody-mindedness, after it had been made clear that her grandmother's presence would *not* be welcomed there by the St Claire family.

Out of sheer stubbornness she had decided to represent her own family that day, standing at the back of the church to mourn her Grandpa Alex. Unacknowledged and thankfully unnoticed by any of the St Claire family.

The coldly remote Lucan St Claire had been easily recognisable from the photographs Lexie had deliberately looked out for over the last few years in the business pages of newspapers and magazines. She had also known the youngest St Claire brother, the rakishly handsome actor Jordan Sinclair, which had to make the austerely attractive blond-haired man standing beside him his twin brother Gideon.

But Lexie's grandmother—the woman Alexander St Claire had loved and shared the last seventeen years of his life with—had been absent from his funeral…

For that alone Lexie would never forgive *any* of the St Claire family. The head of that family, especially. Lucan St Claire. The man who, upon his father's death, had become the fifteenth Duke of Stourbridge.

Not that Lucan St Claire ever used the title. No doubt as some further insult to the father he had all but disowned twenty-five years ago.

Lexie's eyes snapped her resentment now, as she looked up at Lucan St Claire. 'Can I help you with something else, Mr St Claire…?'

Lucan didn't believe himself to be a vain man. He recognized that he was cold, occasionally ruthless and that other than with his close family he was almost always chillingly remote. He was also aware that it was as much his considerable wealth and power that attracted all those models and actresses to him as any personal attraction he might or might not have.

That aside, Lexie Hamilton's initial attitude of dismissal, followed by this disdain, were not things Lucan had ever encountered in any other woman.

Intriguingly so...

'Are you always this disrespectful?' he rasped harshly.

She shrugged. 'My parents brought me up to believe that respect has to be earned, not just given,' she came back challengingly.

Lucan growled something unintelligible under his breath. 'I want you to sit in on my ten o'clock meeting and take notes.'

'Well, that *is* what you are paying me for,' she came back sarcastically.

Lucan's patience—what little he possessed—was fast running out where this particular woman was concerned. 'If you continue with your present attitude you will leave me with no choice but to call your agency back and explain exactly how ill-suited I believe you to be for this or any other position,' he warned her coldly.

Lexie grudgingly acknowledged that she might be allowing her inner resentment towards this man to get the better of her. After all, he *was* Lucan St Claire, world-renowned businessman, and a man who was rich as Croesus and even more powerful. The last thing Lexie wanted was for her parents to return from their cruise and discover the hard-earned reputation of Premier Personnel, which they had so painstakingly built up over the last twenty years, was in tatters after only a matter of days under Lexie's management!

'Shouldn't you at least give me a few hours to prove my efficiency before doing that?' she came back lightly.

Even when this woman was saying all the right words

she still somehow managed to sound challenging, Lucan recognised with a frown. Almost as if she had been pre-disposed to dislike him…

Simply because of the unfeeling way she believed he had behaved towards Jessica Brown?

Or was her dislike for another reason entirely?

Considering that Lexie Hamilton hadn't even known Lucan's ex-PA, the former didn't sound like an acceptable explanation for her attitude. So maybe it was something else?

Or perhaps it wasn't personal at all, and she really was just this prickly and outspoken with everyone?

If he could tolerate this woman in such close proximity to him for the next three days he was probably going to find that out.

And he still had to decide what he was going to do about John Barton's call concerning the damage to Mulberry Hall…

'Is there something wrong, Mr St Claire?' Lexie prompted lightly a couple of hours later, once Gideon St Claire had left the office to accompany Andrew Proctor and his legal representative down in the lift.

'What could possibly be wrong?' Lucan bit out tautly as he stood up impatiently, a nerve pulsing in his tightly clenched jaw. He moved around the desk, the darkness of his gaze narrowed on her icily.

Lexie gave a shake of her head. 'I had assumed you might offer to take Mr Proctor out to lunch once the con-tracts had been signed—'

'I believe Proctor would much rather have had lunch with *you* than with me.'

'Me?' Lexie repeated incredulously.

'Don't play the innocent with me, Lexie; you know

exactly what effect you had on Andrew Proctor,' he growled scathingly.

She frowned. 'I believe I laughed at several of Mr Proctor's jokes—'

'Laughed inappropriately at *all* of his jokes,' Lucan corrected disgustedly, fresh anger boiling up inside him just at the thought of the meeting that had just taken place in his office.

Andrew Proctor was a handsome man in his late forties, owner of an extensive transport business that Lucan wished to acquire for the St Claire Corporation. There had been several meetings between Gideon and Proctor's own legal adviser already, to negotiate the details of the sale, and Lucan had fully expected the meeting this morning—the signing of the contracts—to go off without a hitch.

Obviously he hadn't taken Lexie's presence into account when he'd made that assumption!

Andrew Proctor had taken one glance at Lucan's PA and the whole tenor of the meeting had changed. The man had begun to flirt with her instead of paying attention to the final discussion of the contract that had been drawn up for their signatures.

The fact that Gideon had seemed equally interested in her certainly hadn't improved the situation.

Lucan's mouth tightened. 'You all but got into bed with the man, damn it!'

Lexie's eyes widened indignantly. 'Believe me, Mr St Claire, when I get into bed with a man I *don't* do it in front of an audience!'

Lucan drew in a sharp breath at the graphic vision that remark instantly induced.

Her complexion was pure ivory, and Lucan had no doubt that the slenderness of her body would be just as palely translucent. Her skin would be soft and smooth to the touch. Her uptilted breasts would be tipped by rose or red-coloured nipples. The silky triangle of hair between her legs would be the same dark—

Good God!

Had he totally lost his mind? Christmas in Scotland, followed by the wedding at Mulberry Hall and now this call from Barton in Gloucestershire—all that had been unsettling, certainly, but surely not enough to addle Lucan's brain so much he was having these erotic thoughts about her?

Addled his brain?

It was another part of his anatomy entirely that responded to Lexie's exotic beauty.

'I have no interest in learning what you do or do not require when you go to bed with a man,' he bit out grimly—and not altogether truthfully. 'I am merely endeavouring to point out that your overtly friendly behaviour towards Andrew Proctor made a complete fiasco of what was supposed to be a business meeting.'

Lexie was uncomfortably aware that Lucan's criticism was partly merited. She had obviously been expected to just fade quietly into the background of the meeting, rather than allow Andrew Proctor to draw her into conversation. And she knew she would have done exactly that if not for the fact that she had seen exactly how annoyed Lucan had looked every time Andrew Proctor spoke to her...

She gave a self-conscious grimace now. 'I apologise if you found anything about my behaviour this morning less than professional.'

Lucan looked taken aback. '*What* did you just say...?'

Lexie shot him a frowning glance from beneath dark lashes. 'I believe I apologised,' she repeated impatiently.

Exactly what Lucan had thought she had done! Totally

unexpectedly. So much so that he wasn't quite sure what to do or say next, damn it.

Indecision wasn't something he could normally be accused of, either.

What was wrong with him this morning?

From a professional angle Lucan knew he should call this woman's agency and demand that she be replaced immediately, or he would have no choice but to contact another agency.

What he personally wanted to do was another matter entirely...

He relaxed slightly. 'It's almost one o'clock. I suggest the two of us go and get some lunch—'

'Together?' Lexie stared at him uncomprehendingly.

'Yes—together,' Lucan drawled mockingly. 'Perhaps we can come to some sort of truce while we eat?'

To say Lexie was stunned by the suggestion would be an understatement. Unless Lucan meant it as an ultimatum rather than a suggestion? An implication that the two of them either come to that truce or he would immediately go ahead with his threat to have her replaced, and in doing so damage the reputation of Premier Personnel?

Personally, Lexie would be more than happy to go. She had already done what she'd come here to do, and that was to meet Lucan St Claire and have all her preconceived ideas of him confirmed. As well as some *un*preconceived ones—namely, he was dangerously attractive...

Unfortunately, the repercussions for Premier Personnel if that were to happen were less acceptable.

Something Lexie should definitely have thought about before acting so impulsively in coming anywhere near a single member of the St Claire family!

Although, Lexie acknowledged grudgingly, she hadn't

found the blond and handsome Gideon St Claire quite so disagreeable as Lucan.

Gideon was supposed to share the same reputation for coldness and arrogance as his haughty older brother, and as such Lexie had fully expected him to ignore her altogether during this morning's meeting. Instead, Gideon had been effortlessly charming to her, and the warm interest in his gaze unmistakable…

'Does it usually take you this long to respond to an invitation to lunch?' Lucan rasped impatiently.

'No, of course not,' Lexie snapped resentfully, her cheeks heating at the taunting mockery she could see in those coal-black eyes. 'But it was hardly an invitation, was it?' she dismissed scathingly. ''More like, it's lunchtime, so let's eat!'

Lucan frowned his irritation; did this woman have to argue about everything? 'I see nothing wrong with that statement,' he bit out impatiently. 'It *is* lunchtime, and we both have to eat.'

'But not necessarily together,' she came back decisively.

Lucan's eyes narrowed to dark and dangerous slits. 'Tell me—is this dislike personal, or do you treat all your employers with the same contempt?'

Lexie stiffened warily. It was one thing for her to treat Lucan St Claire with the disdain she felt he deserved—quite another for him to become overly curious as to *why* she treated him that way. For him to ever suspect, realise, exactly who she was…

Lexie shook her head. 'It isn't personal, Mr St Claire—'

'Lucan.'

She blinked up at him. 'I beg your pardon…?'

'I invited you to call me Lucan, Lexie,' he drawled ruefully. 'Don't tell me you have a problem with that, too?' He frowned again as she continued to stare up at him.

Of *course* Lexie had a problem with that! The last thing she wanted—positively the last thing—was to be on a first-name basis with any of the arrogant St Claire family! 'I would prefer to keep our relationship on a completely business footing,' she said stiffly.

'And calling each other by our first names isn't doing that?' he prompted.

'You know it isn't.' She frowned. 'Any more than my having lunch with you is,' she added coolly.

Lucan scowled his impatience. 'I fail to see why not.'

Lexie eyed him frustratedly. 'That could be because you're being deliberately obtuse—' She broke off abruptly as he gave a wry chuckle.

A phenomenon that completely changed the austerity of those grimly handsome features, giving warmth to those dark, dark eyes, a softening to the hard rigidity of his cheek and jawline, and revealing an endearing cleft in his left cheek.

All things that Lexie did not want to be aware of where this particular man was concerned.

She gave him a reproving look. 'I fail to see what's so funny.'

He gave a rueful shake of his head. 'It seems that even when you try to be polite you can't help but be rude.'

She bristled. 'And you find that amusing?'

'Not really.' He gave a slow shake of his head. 'I've just never met anyone quite like you before,' he said.

Lexie wasn't sure she was altogether comfortable with the softening of his tone. Or the speculation she could see in the warmth of those dark eyes as he looked at her. It was too male an assessment. The assessment of a handsome man looking at a woman he found attractive…

No way!

Absolutely no way!

Lucan St Claire and his two brothers had all but disowned their own father after he and their mother were divorced. Had totally rejected so much as even meeting the woman their father had loved and spent the rest of his life with.

Lexie accepted that their parents' divorce must have been tough on three young boys such as Lucan and his two brothers would have been twenty-five years ago. But they *had* been only boys, and as such couldn't possibly have been aware of all the details of the situation.

Any more than Lexie, who hadn't even been born at the time, could really know...

No, she wasn't even going there.

The whole of the St Claire family had treated Grandpa Alex and her grandmother abominably as far as she was concerned. As such, they were all beneath contempt. It was better for Lexie if she continued to think that way.

Except, as she had realised this morning, Lucan St Claire was lethally and heart-poundingly handsome.

Lucan had seen some of the emotions flickering across Lexie's expressive, beautiful face. Seen them, but not understood them. Which wasn't so unusual; so far there was very little about this woman that he *did* understand.

Except that for some inexplicable reason he was attracted to her.

Her outward beauty was undeniable, but it was the things Lucan didn't know about her, the things he didn't yet understand, that intrigued him.

And that, if Lucan were completely honest with himself, was also the reason he had been so annoyed at Andrew Proctor's flirting with her earlier.

He straightened abruptly. 'I take it from your earlier remarks that you would prefer to give lunch a miss?'

She frowned. 'Not completely, no...'

'Just lunch with *me*?' Lucan guessed easily.

Her mouth tightened. 'Yes.'

It was all Lucan could do to stop himself from laughing again. No woman had ever before given him the blunt put-downs that Lexie did so effortlessly!

Put-downs he found more arousing than annoying when they were coming from between Lexie's full and sensually erotic lips...

He gave a terse nod of his head. 'I had thought you might appreciate having lunch before we leave. But we can eat later if that's what you would prefer.'

'Before we leave for where?' Lexie said slowly, suspiciously, not liking the gleam of satisfaction she could clearly see in the depths of Lucan's dark eyes.

Eyes that now met hers with mocking innocence. 'Did I forget to mention we're leaving town for a couple of days?'

Lexie very much doubted that this man ever forgot anything—after sitting in on this morning's meeting, witnessing the precision of his business acumen as he rattled off reams of facts and figures without consulting a single sheet of paper in Andrew Proctor's file, Lexie no longer believed he had forgotten his previous PA's name, either. A more logical explanation for that oversight was that the woman had simply been of such insignificance to him that he simply hadn't troubled himself to learn it.

He didn't seem to be having the same trouble where *she* was concerned.

'Yes...' Lexie confirmed warily.

He nodded tersely. 'I finally managed to return Barton's call earlier. After careful consideration I've decided that

I *should* go to Gloucestershire to deal with the problem personally after all.'

Lexie's heart gave a sickening lurch. 'And this affects me how?'

Those dark eyes glittered down at her with mocking satisfaction. 'I would have thought that was obvious, Lexie.'

'Humour me, Mr St Claire,' she bit out between gritted teeth.

He shrugged those broad shoulders beneath his tailored jacket. 'For the next three days you work for me. I need to go to Gloucestershire for the next couple of days at least, to assess the damage to the house there and to organise repairs. Obviously I expect my temporary temporary PA—namely you—to accompany me.'

Lexie felt the colour drain from her cheeks as she stared up at him in stunned disbelief.

Lucan wanted her to accompany him to Gloucestershire? To Mulberry Hall? The St Claire ducal estate in the village of Stourbridge?

The same village where Lexie's grandmother still lived…

CHAPTER THREE

LUCAN couldn't help but see the way Lexie reacted as he outlined his plans for spending the next couple of days in Gloucestershire; her eyes had become dark and haunted, her cheeks deathly pale.

Obviously Lucan had a personal aversion to going anywhere near the family estate—which was the reason he had decided to take this intriguing woman with him—but he saw no reason why she should feel the same way. Unless, of course, she had personal commitments that kept her in town—maybe a boyfriend or a live-in lover?

'Do you have a problem with that?' he rasped harshly.

Did Lexie have a problem with that?

She couldn't even begin to list the problems she had with going anywhere near the village of Stourbridge in the company of this particular man. With Lucan St Claire. The head of the despised St Claire family.

Lexie had been visiting the village of Stourbridge for years, of course, on frequent visits to her grandmother and Grandpa Alex. As a child she had gone there with her parents, and latterly on her own. Stourbridge was a delightful village, full of charming thatched cottages, and Lexie always enjoyed spending time there with her grandmother.

Which was the pertinent point, of course.

To go anywhere near Stourbridge, the village where Lexie had been known by many of the locals from the time she was a baby, with Lucan St Claire of all people, was simply asking for trouble.

Oh, what a tangled web...

And that web had just become more tangled than Lexie could ever have imagined when she had allowed curiosity to get the better of her!

Her throat moved convulsively as she swallowed hard, and her gaze avoided meeting that probing dark one as instead she looked somewhere over Lucan's left shoulder. 'I can't simply up and leave London at a moment's notice...'

'I've already checked with your agency, and part of your contract of employment states that you agree to accompany your employer in the course of his/her business,' Lucan informed her coldly.

Having worked at the agency alongside her parents for the last three years, Lexie knew exactly what the Premier Personnel contract said concerning their expectations of employees. As the daughter of the owners of the company it was also a contract *she* hadn't signed—a fact Lexie obviously couldn't share with him.

Her mouth firmed. 'Your reasons for going to Gloucestershire appear to be personal rather than business-related.'

'Correct me if I'm wrong—' his icily taunting tone implied that he already knew he wasn't '—but I believe the initials PA stand for Personal Assistant...?'

'Yes. But—'

'In which case, as you are my PA, I fully expect you to accompany me to Gloucestershire.'

'I disagree—'

'And do you believe that your opinion on the subject is of *any* relevance to me?' he cut in brutally.

Lexie looked at Lucan searchingly, easily noting the hard glitter of those dark eyes, the pulse pounding in his rigidly clenched jaw, the thin, uncompromising line of his mouth. 'No,' she finally acknowledged heavily. 'But surely this visit could wait until my replacement takes over on Thursday?' she added brightly.

'I have no intention of altering my plans to suit you, Lexie,' he bit out coldly. 'If it makes you feel any better, I shall be taking a briefcase full of work with me.'

'Oh…' She gave a pained grimace.

That ruthless mouth twisted into a humourless smile as he nodded haughtily. 'I'll expect you back here in an hour, then, with your case duly packed.'

Lexie could feel the panic rising inside her. She *couldn't* go to the St Claire estate in Gloucestershire with this man. She simply couldn't!

Her grandmother's cottage was only half a mile away from Mulberry Hall, the majestic mansion that was the St Claire ducal home. Lexie had played in the woods there when she was a child, had taken long walks in the grounds with her grandmother and Grandpa Alex, had often used the indoor swimming pool that had been built onto the back of Mulberry Hall.

Admittedly Lexie had never stayed at Mulberry Hall itself, her grandmother having always refused to live there with Alexander even after his divorce, but Lexie knew she would only have to make one slip, one remark that revealed she had been inside the house or on the estate before, for Lucan to demand an explanation. An explanation she had no intention of giving him.

This wasn't just a tangled web, it was a steel trap, waiting to snap shut behind her.

Lexie gave a firm shake of her head. 'I really would prefer not to accompany you to Gloucestershire—'

'In that case,' he interrupted grimly, 'I have no doubt that Premier Personnel will have no choice but to dispense with your services altogether. For their own sake.'

'Are you threatening me, Mr St Claire?' Lexie snapped, easily able to guess what that meant. This man had the power and influence to totally ruin Premier Personnel's reputation in the business world with only a few cutting words.

Something Lexie should definitely have thought of earlier.

'I haven't even begun to threaten you yet, Lexie,' he assured her succinctly.

There was no mistaking the hard implacability of that coal-black gaze—an indication that Lucan was determined to have his own way. What Lexie didn't understand was why. Why was he was so set on her accompanying him to Gloucestershire when she so obviously didn't want to go?

Unless that was the very reason Lucan was being so insistent?

This man was hard, cold, ruthless. A man used to people doing exactly as he wanted them to. Who insisted on it. By arguing with him Lexie had no doubt she was just making Lucan all the more determined to bend her to his indomitable will.

And Lexie, fool that she was, had placed herself—and Premier Personnel—in a position where she could do nothing to stop him.

Her eyes glittered her dislike as she glared up at him. 'An hour, I believe you said?'

Lucan felt absolutely no satisfaction in having forced Lexie to his will. Just as he had absolutely no idea what thoughts had been going through that beautiful head while Lexie deliberated as to whether or not she was going to do as he asked. But whatever those thoughts had been they didn't appear to have been particularly pleasant ones…

He couldn't read this woman at all—which was unusual in itself; most women of his acquaintance seemed intent on either sharing his bed or attempting to get him to the altar. Usually with an avaricious eye on the fortune and power he had amassed these last ten years.

Lexie Hamilton made it obvious she was unimpressed with both him and his obvious wealth, and behaved towards him accordingly. Namely, she treated him with an offhand disdain that—contrary to what she'd obviously hoped—had only succeeded in increasing his interest in her.

Enough so that he welcomed the distraction of her presence, unwilling or otherwise, during this forced second visit to Mulberry Hall in as many weeks.

'An hour,' he confirmed abruptly.

She nodded. 'Would you like me to find out the times of the trains?'

'I intend driving up,' Lucan dismissed. 'Normally we would have flown up in the company-owned helicopter, but it's being serviced at the moment.'

The St Claires really were a breed apart, Lexie decided slightly dazedly. Super-rich. Super-powerful.

How on earth her gentle and unassuming grandmother had ever dared to fall in love with the head of that rich and powerful family was a wonder in itself!

'Silly me.' Lexie grimaced.

He nodded. 'You should pack warm clothing—'

'I believe I'm intelligent enough to have worked that out for myself,' she snapped in her irritation.

'I don't think I've ever given you reason to think I believe you lacking in intelligence, Lexie,' he assured her huskily.

'So far,' she challenged.

'Ever,' Lucan corrected gruffly.

Lexie looked at him uncertainly, slightly unnerved by the throaty huskiness of his tone, and even more so by what she could see in those dark eyes as Lucan steadily returned her gaze.

Dear Lord, she was going away with this man for two days. Would be in his company for the same amount of time. Constantly in his disturbing company…!

'I'll be back within the hour,' she confirmed.

But first Lexie had to go to the office of Premier Personnel and explain the situation to Brenda.

Attempt to explain something Lexie couldn't fully explain to herself!

'Put your seat belt on,' Lucan advised as he turned on the ignition of his black Range Rover.

Lexie had looked disturbingly attractive when she'd returned to the offices of the St Claire Corporation an hour or so ago, carrying a thick calf-length woollen coat and an overnight bag, and dressed in a blue sweater the same colour as her eyes, with denims that fitted snugly over that shapely bottom and slender legs before being tucked into calf-high boots. The long length of that gloriously wild black hair was secured in a loose plait down her spine, revealing that she wore small pearls in the lobes of her ears. An oval gold locket was also visible against the blue of her sweater.

Closed in the confines of the Range Rover with her, Lucan was also aware of the subtleness of the perfume she wore, along with a softer, even more subtle smell that was provocatively feminine. In fact the small and very womanly bundle beside him was—as Lucan had hoped she would be—a distraction from the fact that their destination was Mulberry Hall.

Although Lucan knew that no one, and nothing, would ever make him feel completely relaxed about returning to the house he had lived in until he was eleven years old.

Lucan knew from attending Jordan's wedding almost a week ago that the house had changed little since he'd last spent any time there. There was no reason for it to have done. The furnishings and draperies were antiques, the floors downstairs mainly marble, the paintings on the walls originals, as were the ornamental statues, and the impressive chandeliers that hung from the high ceilings were of very old Venetian glass.

No, there was no doubting that Mulberry Hall was a beautiful house. A gracious house. A house fit for a duke. The Duke of Stourbridge. A title Lucan currently held.

Something else he had avoided thinking about for the last eight years.

As the eldest child of a broken marriage Lucan had found it all too easy to blame Mulberry Hall and the demands of holding the title of Duke of Stourbridge, as much as his father's and Sian Thomas's affair, for wrecking his parents' marriage and creating a schism in his own young life and that of his brothers. Lucan wanted to avoid all of those things. Mulberry Hall. His father. The title of Duke. Most of all, Sian Thomas—the woman Alexander had loved enough to sacrifice his whole family for…

Initially, after the divorce was over and emotions had calmed somewhat, Alexander had tried to encourage his three sons to meet and get to know Sian Thomas. An encouragement that had fallen on stony ground as they'd all refused to go anywhere near the woman they held responsible for their parents' separation and divorce.

Damn it, Lucan wouldn't be going near the place again now if John Barton, the caretaker, hadn't made it so obvious that he thought Lucan should see the damage to the house for himself.

Lucan had insisted on Lexie Hamilton coming with him because he had hoped her sharp-tongued presence would be enough of a diversion for him to repress these grim and disturbing thoughts—at least until he actually reached Gloucestershire and could no longer avoid them!

A scowling glance in her direction showed Lucan that she was, in fact, gazing out of the side window of the car as they drove out of London, obviously enjoying the winter wonderland England had become following yet another heavy snowfall two days earlier. The roads had been cleared, at least, but the countryside was still covered in a thick layer of cold and haunting beauty.

Those blue sooty-lashed eyes were bright with pleasure when Lexie turned to return his gaze. 'Everywhere looks so beautiful when it's covered in snow, doesn't it?'

Lucan's mouth twisted derisively. 'Much like papering over the cracks in life and hoping no one will notice!'

Lexie frowned slightly as she became aware of Lucan's obvious tension. 'It doesn't have to be like that.'

He gave a weary sigh. '*Please* tell me you aren't one of those people whose glass is always half-full rather than half-empty?'

Lexie felt her cheeks warm at Lucan's obvious derision. 'It's preferable to being a cynic!'

'I prefer to think of myself as a realist,' he rasped.

'Which is just a polite way of saying you're a cynic,' she dismissed.

He gave her a derisive glance. 'I don't believe that politeness is exactly your forte, Lexie!'

'Or yours!' she came back tartly.

'True,' Lucan murmured softly.

Lexie gave him a sharp glance. 'Don't tell me we actually agree on something?'

'Unusual, but the answer to that would appear to be yes,' he drawled ruefully.

'Wow!'

'Wow, indeed,' Lucan echoed dryly. 'This is going to be a long drive, Lexie, so why don't you pass some of the time away by telling me a little about yourself?' he encouraged.

Lexie stiffened warily. Lucan wanted her to tell him about herself? Such as what? Who her parents were? Her grandmother?

Every part of Lexie's life was a minefield of facts that, if revealed, would probably result in Lucan stopping the car right now and simply throwing her out into this stark and snow-covered landscape!

Which wasn't an altogether bad idea, considering the circumstances...

She moistened dry lips. 'Why don't you tell me about yourself instead?'

His mouth tightened. 'Perhaps we should just put on some music?'

Lexie slowly breathed her relief that Lucan wasn't going to insist on pursuing the subject of herself. It was also interesting to realise that Lucan was as reluctant to talk about himself as she was...

She couldn't help wondering why that was. Surely the life of Lucan St Claire, billionaire entrepreneur, was pretty much an open book? The business life of billionaire entrepreneur Lucan St Claire, maybe, but obviously there were things about his private life that Lucan preferred not to talk about.

His reticence instantly made Lexie wonder exactly what those things could be.

Perhaps a woman…?

She looked at him from beneath ebony lashes. The darkness of his hair really would look more attractive if worn a little longer, and the bleak expression in those almost black eyes as he concentrated on driving was off-putting, but neither of those things detracted from the fact that his was a magnetically handsome face. As for the leashed power of that taut and obviously toned body—

Oh, please, no…!

Lexie recoiled with inward horror. She had only wanted to meet Lucan St Claire—to see for herself how cold and ruthless he was. Becoming physically aware of him, actually finding him attractive, had *not* been part of her plan.

As much as accompanying Lucan to Mulberry Hall in Gloucestershire hadn't been part of Lexie's plan…

'What sort of music do you like?'

Lexie blinked before focusing on Lucan with effort. 'Classical, mostly.' She shrugged.

Dark brows rose over those almost black eyes as he glanced at her. 'Really?'

'Yes, really,' she confirmed sharply. 'Did you imagine I might like heavy rock or something?' she added scathingly.

'Not at all. I'm just surprised that we have the same taste in music, that's all.' He reached forward to switch on the radio, and the car was instantly filled with the soft and haunting strains of Mozart.

It would *have* to be Mozart!

Her grandmother's favourite composer.

Lexie had occasionally stayed with Nanna Sian on her own for several weeks during the school summer holidays when she was growing up and her parents had had to work.

Weeks when Mozart would invariably be playing on the CD player her grandmother kept in the kitchen.

In the kitchen of the cottage where her grandmother still lived—which was only half a mile away from Mulberry Hall…

Lexie was starting to feel ill—and it had nothing to do with travel sickness.

'Perhaps when we get there you'll find the damage to the house in Gloucestershire isn't as bad as Mr Barton thinks it is and we'll be able to return to town tomorrow?' she said hopefully.

Lucan glanced at Lexie from between narrowed lids as he heard almost a note of desperation in her voice. Because she didn't want to spend a couple of days in rural Gloucestershire with him? Or because she had a need to get back to something—someone—in London as soon as possible?

Both of those explanations were somehow unsatisfactory to Lucan.

'And perhaps I'll find it's worse than I thought and we'll have to stay for a week,' he drawled mockingly—a remark that resulted in those blue eyes widening slightly in dismay before the emotion was quickly controlled. 'Do you have personal commitments that make being away awkward for you?' Lucan asked, and scowled.

'Personal commitments?' She frowned.

'Husband? Live-in-lover? Boyfriend?'

'No, of course not,' she answered irritably.

Lucan relaxed slightly. 'And I'm sure you must have had to go away on business before with your employers?'

'Well… I— Yes. Of course.' She seemed slightly flustered. 'It's just—I'm only supposed to be working for you for a total of three days,' she reminded him tersely.

'I'm sure your agency will understand if our return

is delayed for any reason,' Lucan growled unsympathetically.

'I'm not sure that I will!' she came back pertly.

Lucan felt his irritation increasing at Lexie's continuing arguments. Damn it, hadn't his New Year got off to enough of a bad start already without—?

Redirected anger, Lucan recognised grimly. Not that Lexie wasn't infuriating—she undoubtedly was. But Lucan knew it was his own frustration and annoyance at having to return to Mulberry Hall again so soon that was making his mood so volatile. Otherwise Lucan knew he would have put this woman firmly, chillingly, in her place by now.

Except Lucan wasn't completely sure what her place was.

Stretched out naked on his bed, that glorious long dark hair splayed behind her on the pillows as he explored every inch of her silken body with his lips and hands, was the place he could most easily picture her...

Lucan shifted uncomfortably in his seat as he felt himself harden just at imagining kissing every silken inch of her naked body. 'As I believe I have already made clear—several times,' he added grimly, 'your own requirements in this matter are of little importance to me.'

Lexie gave a snort as she shook her head disgustedly. 'With a selfish attitude like that I have no idea why you were in the least surprised when Jessica Brown walked out on you without notice!'

Lucan gave a hard and humourless smile. 'What a pity you aren't in a position to do the same...'

'Isn't it?' Lexie returned, saccharine-sweet.

Really, this man was totally obnoxious. Arrogant. Haughty. Cold. Mocking.

And so darkly attractive he took Lexie's breath away…

Something that certainly wasn't going to help her through the next trying couple of days…

CHAPTER FOUR

'WELL,' Lucan bit out tersely, having climbed out of the Range Rover to pull on his heavy jacket, before moving round to the passenger side of the parked vehicle to open Lexie's door for her.

Lexie's heart was beating a wild tattoo as she slowly got out of the car to look up at the mellow-stoned magnificence that was Mulberry Hall as it towered majestically over the snow-covered grounds of the Stourbridge estate.

A house and estate Lexie was more familiar with than she wanted the man at her side ever to know.

She turned to look up at him challengingly. 'Well, what?'

He raised dark and mocking brows. 'It's been my experience so far in our acquaintance that you usually have something to say about most things…'

Lexie deliberately kept her expression non-committal as she glanced back at Mulberry Hall. 'I'm betting the electricity bills are high!'

Lucan's bark of laughter was completely spontaneous. Something that seemed, surprisingly, to have occurred several times in the company of this particular woman. Rare indeed, Lucan acknowledged ruefully, for a man usually known for his grimness rather than his sense of humour.

Even rarer for Lexie not to have made some sort of

cutting remark on the obvious and exclusive grandeur that was Mulberry Hall…

'Shouldn't we go inside?' she prompted pointedly.

Lucan nodded abruptly. 'Time to assess the damage.' He took a firm hold of Lexie's arm as he glanced up at the blue tarpaulin that had been fixed temporarily over part of the roof of the west wing of the house. 'I wouldn't want you to fall over and break a leg,' he drawled mockingly when she frowned up at him.

'In case I sue you?' she taunted.

'The way this year's gone so far, it's a distinct possibility!' Lucan's other hand reached out instinctively to steady her as she would have slipped on one of the icy steps leading up to the huge front door, the movement turning her slightly and bringing her into close contact with the hardness of his chest.

Lexie stopped breathing as she felt the warmth of his body envelop her. As she became totally aware of the hardness of his chest and abdomen against her breasts, his firmly muscled legs against her much softer ones.

Even the air about them seemed to still in recognition of that awareness. There had been another fresh fall of snow the previous day, and several inches now covered the surrounding countryside, seeming to surround them in eerie silence.

Lexie slowly raised her head. And then wished she hadn't as she was immediately held captive by the intensity of Lucan's dark and fathomless eyes. The stillness of that air about them became charged, heated, as Lexie found herself unable to look away.

Close to, like this, she could see that those eyes were a deep chocolate-brown surrounded by a ring of black. Dark and compelling eyes. Eyes that Lexie knew she could drown in. Deep and fathomless eyes that seemed to turn to the deep brown of hot liquid chocolate as she continued to stare up at him.

Eyes that Lexie suddenly realised were coming closer as Lucan lowered his head and that firm and yet sensual mouth came within touching distance of her own.

Lexie reared back sharply before wrenching her arm out of Lucan's grasp. 'You really don't want to do that!' she warned.

He returned her gaze steadily. 'I don't?'

'No.' She scowled, and had to reach out instinctively to place her hand on the wall at the side of the steps as she felt herself in danger of slipping again.

Lexie might have every reason to despise Lucan St Claire, but she had absolutely no doubt that if he were to kiss her—to kiss the granddaughter of the despised Sian Thomas—Lucan would have reason to dislike himself, too.

What a bitter irony it would be, Lexie realised heavily, if he were to find himself attracted to the very last woman in the world he would ever want to feel such an interest in.

She gave a disgusted shake of her head. 'Do you think you could possibly unlock the door so that we can go inside out of the cold?' she snapped in her impatience.

Lucan drew in a rasping breath. His first for several long seconds, he realised. The whole of the length of time he had held the softness of Lexie's body moulded against the length of his, in fact…

Her breasts beneath her sweater had felt full and lush as they'd pressed against his chest, her thighs in the fitted denims soft and enticing against the hardness of his arousal. Her mouth, those deliciously provocative lips, moist and slightly parted in invitation. An invitation Lucan would have been only too happy to accept. *Would* have accepted, damn it, if Lexie hadn't pulled away so abruptly!

For a few brief moments it had been pleasant to anticipate spending the next two or three days—and nights—dealing with the hunger Lucan seemed to have developed for Lexie's curvaceous softness, rather than with the real reason he was here.

Except there was really no escaping the fact that Mulberry Hall loomed large and overpowering before him…

'Of course.' Lucan's mouth was set grimly as he turned away to climb the last two steps, pausing briefly to draw in a deep and controlling breath before unlocking and pushing open the front door.

Standing in the doorway, looking into the cavernous marble-floored entrance hall, Lucan instantly detected a slightly musty smell that hadn't been there a week ago. An indication that the water damage Lucan had seen on the outside of the building had, as John Barton had already warned, actually entered the house.

The west wing of the house, to be exact, where that damned portrait of his father hung so regally.

With any luck the portrait would be one of the things to have been damaged!

'Lucan…?' Lexie prompted uncertainly as he seemed transfixed in the doorway, apparently as reluctant as she was to actually go inside the house.

'Sorry.' He drew himself up abruptly and stepped aside to allow her to enter.

It felt slightly warmer as Lexie stepped inside, but not much. 'Does anyone actually live here any more?' she turned to ask huskily as she gave an involuntary shiver before wrapping her long coat more tightly about her.

'Not for years.' Lucan's expression was as bleak as his tone of voice as he followed her inside, before closing the door behind him to shut out the icy blast of the cold wind.

'Wait for me here while I go to the back of the house and turn up the heating.' He turned abruptly on his heel and strode off down a hallway without waiting for her to reply.

Not that Lexie had been going to make one. She was as unnerved at being back at Mulberry Hall as Lucan appeared to be.

She huddled further down into her coat as she stood looking around the familiar surroundings. She hadn't actually been inside Mulberry Hall since Grandpa Alex had died, eight years ago, but it didn't look as if anything had changed in that time.

The huge cut-glass Venetian chandelier still hung from the cavernous ceiling overhead, and the two doors directly off the entrance hall led, she knew, into a graciously furnished sitting room and a spacious dining room that would seat at least a dozen people at its long oak table.

Another door further down the hallway opened up into what had once been a mirrored ballroom, big enough to hold a hundred or so guests, but which was now a gym and games room.

Years ago Grandpa Alex had taught a nine-year-old Lexie to play table tennis and billiards in that room, while an indulgent Nanna Sian looked on fondly...

Lexie felt an emotional lump in her throat and an ache in her chest as she remembered the laughter that had filled the bleakness of this house in those days. The same love and laughter there had always been wherever Grandpa Alex and Nanna Sian were together.

A togetherness that Lucan St Claire and the rest of his unforgiving family had wanted no part of.

The same Lucan St Claire who, minutes ago, had been on the verge of kissing Lexie—the granddaughter of the woman he and his family so despised...

Lexie gave another shiver, having absolutely no doubt as to the depth of Lucan's anger if he were ever to realise exactly who she was…

'It should warm up in here shortly,' Lucan rasped as he strode back into the entrance hall. He scowled darkly as Lexie gave an involuntary start, her deep blue eyes wary as she turned sharply to look at him. 'As far as I'm aware we don't have any family ghosts,' he said dryly, mocking her reaction.

She gave him a scathing glance. 'Very funny!'

'I don't believe I've ever been known for my sense of humour, Lexie.'

'I wonder why! Is there some tea or coffee in the kitchen so that I can at least make us a warm drink?'

Lucan arched mocking brows. 'Are you sure that making hot drinks for the two of us comes under the job description of a temporary temporary PA?'

'Probably not,' Lexie dismissed tersely. 'But I'm willing to make an exception on this occasion.'

'That's very generous of you,' Lucan drawled, and had to hold back yet another laugh.

'I thought so, too.' She nodded abruptly.

Lucan couldn't help admiring her attitude. Despite the fact that the family had spent several days here at New Years, no one had actually lived in the house for years. Consequently it wasn't very welcoming, and there were no household servants any more—just the caretaker and his wife, who occasionally came in to check that everything was okay. A lot of women—every single one of the glamorous women Lucan had dated these last ten years or so—would have declared the facilities here unsuitable, even primitive, and immediately demanded to be taken to a hotel. Lexie was obviously made of sterner stuff.

'I'm sure there will be tea and coffee, but no milk,' he told her ruefully.

'Black coffee will be fine,' Lexie assured him briskly, and turned away to walk across the entrance hall towards the back of the house. Only to come to an abrupt halt as she realised her mistake. 'Er—I take it the kitchen *is* back here?' She paused uncertainly.

'The door at the end of the hallway.' Lucan nodded before falling into step behind her.

Lexie was completely aware of Lucan as he followed her into the kitchen, to lean back against one of the oak kitchen cabinets as she prepared the coffee percolator.

And she was still completely aware of how close he had been to kissing her minutes ago. Of how, for a few brief seconds, she had wanted him to kiss her…

Admit it, Lexie, she derided herself, Lucan is like no other man you've ever met. Arrogantly confident, darkly handsome, and most of all, so effortlessly powerful. The man was a *duke,* for goodness' sake. That alone was a potent aphrodisiac without all those other…

Lexie's movements stilled self-consciously as she realised she had been so lost in thought that she hadn't noticed Lucan watching her through narrowed lids as she first filled the percolator with water, before taking ground coffee from the kitchen cabinet and pulling open the appropriate drawer to take out a teaspoon.

Because that was where the coffee and the cutlery had always been kept…

'This is going to take a couple of minutes to prepare, if you have something else you need to be doing.' Lexie sincerely hoped the adage 'offence is the best form of defence' was correct.

Lucan scowled darkly as he realised he had been enjoying watching the movement of Lexie's small and gracefully beautiful hands as she made the coffee, imagining the intensity of pleasure he would feel if those same elegant hands were trailing caressingly over every inch of his naked body...

Hell.

An apt description of the constant state of arousal he seemed to find himself in when in this particular woman's company!

Lucan straightened abruptly. 'I'll go and bring our things in from the car.' And he hoped that the icy-cold wind outside would not only dampen his arousal but also clear his head of the erotic images currently going round and round in his mind!

Lexie watched from beneath sooty lashes as Lucan strode out of the kitchen towards the front of the house, waiting until she heard the soft thud of the door closing behind him before she leant weakly back against one of the kitchen cabinets and closed her eyes.

She really wasn't very good at this. They had only been at Mulberry Hall a matter of minutes, and she had already slipped up twice by knowing where the kitchen was and everything in it.

Perhaps it was as well that she had never actually stayed here in the past; at least the bedrooms and other rooms upstairs would be a complete mystery to her!

Although, just thinking about the bedrooms upstairs was enough to remind her of how she had longed earlier to feel Lucan's mouth on and against hers...

She shouldn't be attracted to Lucan—no, not shouldn't. She *couldn't* be attracted to him!

Lucan was a St Claire. Not just *a* St Claire, but the head of the St Claire family. The same family who had hurt and rejected her beloved Nanna Sian all those years ago, and then again eight years ago, by making it obvious they didn't even want her to attend Grandpa Alex's funeral.

Lexie felt her spine straighten with fresh resolve. She disliked all of the St Claire family intensely for the way they had treated her beloved grandmother, and that included Lucan. Most especially the cold and arrogant Lucan!

Except there had been nothing cold about Lucan earlier when he looked down at her so intently. When Lexie had gazed up into those intense dark eyes and felt as if she were balancing on the edge of a volcano, knowing that the heat would intensify, burn, engulf her completely, if she allowed herself to fall into those fathomless depths...

Even now her breasts felt tight, sensitised, the nipples hard and aching against the soft material of her bra, and she felt a warmth between her thighs, a burning. What would it be like, she wondered, to have that firm and sculptured mouth closing over the tips of her breasts as Lucan suckled her deep into the moist heat of his mouth?

'Brr, it's damned cold out there— Sorry, I thought you were Lucan!' the man who had just entered through the back door of the kitchen grimaced in apology as he turned and saw Lexie.

It wasn't too difficult to guess that the tall and sandy-haired man aged in his mid-thirties was John Barton, the caretaker of Mulberry Hall—the man with a faint Scottish accent she had spoken to on the telephone earlier today.

A man Lexie didn't recognise, and so—thankfully—wouldn't recognise her, either!

'An easy mistake when we look so much alike,' she came back teasingly as she watched him place the box he was carrying on top of one of the kitchen units.

He gave a boyishly endearing grin as he straightened, his eyes a warm and friendly blue as he bundled down into the collar of his thick overcoat. 'Lucan didn't mention he was bringing someone with him...' He eyed her speculatively. 'I'm John Barton, the caretaker,' he introduced himself, and held out his hand in greeting.

Lexie briefly shook that firm and capable hand. 'Lexie,' she supplied economically. Deliberately so. The fewer people who knew that it was Lexie *Hamilton* who had accompanied Lucan to Mulberry Hall, the safer she would feel. 'I'm Mr St Claire's PA,' she said lightly. 'Temporarily,' she added firmly.

And unnecessarily.

Except Lexie somehow needed to reassure herself of that fact after the thoughts she had just been having about Lucan. After she had imagined his lips and mouth against her naked breasts—

Stop it, Lexie, she instructed herself firmly. *Stop it right now!*

She straightened abruptly. 'I'm just making some coffee, but Mr St Claire is outside getting our luggage if you want to join him?' she said dismissively. The curiosity she could see in those friendly blue eyes warned her that John Barton would rather linger in the kitchen for a while and satisfy his curiosity about her than go in search of his employer.

He smiled. 'My wife has sent over a few supplies to see you through.' He indicated the box he had placed on the worktop. 'Milk, bread and butter, cheese—stuff like that. I would have brought it over earlier, but Lucan didn't tell me what time he would be arriving,' he added.

'What a surprise!' Lexie muttered dryly as she crossed the kitchen to inspect the box of groceries. As well as the supplies John had mentioned there was also a promising-looking covered glass dish, filled with some sort of meat casserole. Her eyes glowed with pleasure as she turned back to John Barton. 'Please thank your wife—'

'Cathy,' he supplied lightly.

Lexie had been occasional friends with a girl in the village called Cathy when she was growing up. Not enough for the two of them to have remained in touch once they went off to different universities at eighteen, but enough for Lexie's grandmother to write and tell her that Cathy had married the previous year.

But there was no reason to think it was the same Cathy. No doubt John Barton's wife was as Scottish as he was...

'Do you both come from around here?' Lexie prompted conversationally as she studiously began to take the supplies from the box.

'Obviously I'm originally from Scotland.' John Barton gave a rueful smile. 'But Cathy's a local girl—from the village,' he added lightly. 'I expect she'll pop over to say hello to you both sometime tomorrow—'

'I don't think Mr St Claire is planning on staying for very long,' Lexie cut in sharply. Dear God, it probably *was* the same Cathy!

Blonde-haired, green-eyed Cathy, whom Lexie had no doubt made the amiable John Barton as wonderful a wife as he made *her* a loving husband!

'I believe I said we would probably be here for a couple of days at least, Lexie.'

She turned sharply to face Lucan as he filled the doorway into the main house, heavy lids lowered over those dark eyes as he returned her gaze challengingly. Lexie swallowed hard before speaking. 'Mr Barton has very kindly brought over some milk and other supplies.'

'Just the basics,' the other man explained as he crossed the kitchen. 'Sorry this business had to bring you back so soon, Lucan.'

'No problem, John,' Lucan lied as he shook the other man's hand warmly. 'I was thinking of taking Lexie to the

Rose and Crown for dinner this evening, so I'm hoping they still serve meals?'

'Mr Barton's wife has very kindly provided us with a casserole for this evening,' Lexie put in quickly.

The Rose and Crown pub in the village was another place she had no intention of going while she was here; Bill and Mary Collins, the landlord and his wife, were both well aware of exactly who she was, and of her connection to Sian Thomas.

One thing Lexie was now absolutely sure of: she had to go down to the village and visit her grandmother in person, before there was even a possibility of Nanna Sian hearing from anyone else that her granddaughter was currently staying at Mulberry Hall with Lucan St Claire!

CHAPTER FIVE

'I WOULDN'T have thought preparing dinner came under the heading of your duties as a PA, either?' Lucan prompted softly an hour or so later, when he returned to the kitchen after seeing John out and then returning upstairs briefly to change out of his suit. A kitchen which was now filled with the wonderful aroma of the thick and meaty casserole visibly warming through the glass door of the oven.

Blue eyes snapped with irritation as Lexie looked up from where she sat, drinking coffee at the weathered oak table. 'Technically Cathy Barton prepared it. I just put it in the oven to warm.'

'Even so…'

'Oh, stop being so pedantic, Lucan!' She stood up impatiently to pour coffee into a second mug.

'Pedantic…?' Lucan repeated softly.

'Yes, pedantic!' Lexie thrust the coffee mug into his hand. 'Milk and sugar are on the table.' She sat down in her chair to continue staring down into her own coffee mug.

Lucan looked down at that bent dark head as he sipped the black and unsweetened coffee he preferred; his absence obviously hadn't done anything to improve her mood as she didn't look at him or speak. The latter was an unusual occurrence in itself!

Lucan pulled out the chair opposite hers and sat down

to stretch his long legs out under the table. 'What would you be doing now if you were back in London…?'

Lexie eyed him from beneath her lashes, very aware that Lucan had changed out of his formal suit, shirt and tie since she'd last seen him, and now looked more comfortable—and more darkly, devastatingly attractive—in a thick black sweater and fitted black denims. 'Deciding whether to order Chinese or Indian take-out, probably.'

'You can take the girl out of the city but not the city out of the girl, hmm?' he mused softly.

She bristled. 'What's *that* supposed to mean?'

Lucan noted that several wispy strands of that glorious long black hair had come loose from the confining plait, adding a vulnerability to Lexie's heart-shaped face and the long length of her creamy throat. Except, as Lucan knew only too well, Lexie Hamilton had the vulnerability of a spitting cat!

He shrugged. 'I was just attempting to make conversation.'

She frowned. 'Did you decide on what to do about the damage upstairs?'

He nodded. 'I've arranged for a builder to come out and take a look in the morning.'

'And then we can leave?' She looked hopeful.

Lucan grimaced. 'I won't know until the builder has assessed the damage.' He frowned as she still looked disgruntled. 'I realise the facilities aren't too good here. Would you be more comfortable if I organised a couple of rooms for us tonight at the village pub?'

'*No!* I mean—that won't be necessary,' Lexie spoke more calmly when she saw the way Lucan's eyes narrowed at her unnecessary vehemence. 'The house is quite warm now, and we have Cathy Barton's casserole for dinner…'

'Yes…' Lucan acknowledged slowly.

Suspiciously?

Lexie couldn't say she would blame Lucan if he *did* feel a little suspicious when she was reacting so jumpily to almost everything he said. Although it was a little difficult for her not to be that way, when she constantly felt as if her identity as Sian Thomas's granddaughter was going to be exposed at any moment. Especially now that there was a possibility of Lucan's caretaker being married to Cathy Wilson—someone who knew exactly who Lexie was.

Maybe she should just come out with the truth now and get it over and done with?

Oh, yes—and no doubt find herself cast into the dungeon below.

Lexie had been repelled, and a little fascinated, too, when years ago Grandpa Alex had been persuaded into showing her the dungeon hidden behind the huge wine cellar in the basement of the house. A small structure, probably only six feet deep by ten feet wide, its walls, floor and ceiling were made of solid stone four feet thick. The fourth wall was a metal door with one-inch-solid metal bars that had been driven deep down into the stone floor.

She had wondered all those years ago, as she'd stood looking at that impregnable structure, what the past inhabitants of that stone and metal cell could possibly have done to merit being cast into such a lightless and virtually airless prison.

Right now Lexie couldn't help wondering if deliberately deceiving the current Duke of Stourbridge would be considered crime enough...

So, yes, she obviously had the option of coming clean—of telling Lucan exactly who she was. But it was a disclosure that would no doubt make the contempt Lexie had faced this morning—when Lucan had believed her behaviour towards Andrew Proctor to be unprofessional—seem like child's play in comparison.

Had some part of her always relished Lucan knowing who she was? Wanted to somehow spring that knowledge on him, like a magician bringing a rabbit out of a hat, and then enjoy watching Lucan squirm?

If so, then Lexie knew she didn't feel that way any longer. Just a few hours in Lucan's company had been enough to tell her she would be the one who came out worst in any springing of her relationship to Sian Thomas on him!

She stood up abruptly to cross the kitchen and stand near the warmth of the oven. As far away from Lucan as it was possible to get in the confines of what was actually a cavernous kitchen, but seemed to be getting steadily smaller and smaller by the second...

'What would *you* be doing now if you were in London? Out with a beautiful woman, dining at some exclusive restaurant, no doubt?' she prompted derisively.

Lucan studied Lexie's flushed and challenging face for several long seconds. There was something about the way her gaze refused to meet his and the husky tone of her voice that told him that wasn't what she had intended saying. That she was deliberately trying to irritate him.

'I *am* with a beautiful woman,' he pointed out softly. 'And Cathy's casserole smells better than anything I could buy in a restaurant—exclusive or otherwise,' he added ruefully, effectively cutting off the scathing comment he was sure had been about to come out of Lexie's sexy mouth at his compliment; there was nothing she could say after his last comment that wouldn't sound rude to Cathy Barton's generosity!

Instead she turned away and began busying herself getting out the plates and cutlery they would need to eat.

'The casserole is ready to serve now. I was just waiting for you.'

Lucan stood up. 'Would you like some red wine to go with it?'

'Not enough for you to have to bother going down to the cellar and—' She broke off, her eyes wide as she turned sharply to face him. 'At least, I presume that's where you keep your wine?' she added offhandedly.

'Some of it.' Lucan gave a slow inclination of his head, his narrowed gaze still fixed intently on Lexie's slightly pale face. 'But there's probably a bottle or two of red in the back of the food pantry.'

'You don't come here very often, do you?' Once again Lexie decided that offence was the best form of defence if she wanted to deflect Lucan's attention from the fact that she had made yet another slip by mentioning knowing there was a cellar at Mulberry Hall.

'Actually, I attended my brother's wedding here a week ago,' he dismissed. 'And if that was a pick up line then you didn't say it quite right...' He quirked dark and mocking brows.

As if! Only a woman who didn't mind playing with fire would even *think* of becoming involved with Lucan St Claire. Which was a strange thing for Lexie to have thought, considering she had initially thought him so icily cold...

The truth was that Lexie was having trouble continuing to see Lucan that way. How could she think of him as cold when she was still totally aware of the warmth that had emanated from him earlier? Of the feeling as if she were standing on the edge of a volcano that was threatening to erupt and engulf her in its heat?

Outwardly, there was no doubting that Lucan was a cold and arrogant man, but beneath that coldness Lexie realised there was a powerful force. A physical energy that was overwhelming in its intensity.

Much like a magnet, drawing Lexie slowly but surely towards him…

And she didn't want to be drawn to Lucan—recognised only too well the danger of such an attraction.

'I don't have a pick up line, Mr St Claire,' she assured him coldly as she took the casserole from the oven. 'And even if I did I certainly wouldn't use it on you!' she added derisively.

Instantly she realised her mistake, as instead of lessening the tension between them it suddenly seemed to become thicker, almost palpable.

Lucan's eyes had narrowed to black slits. 'Why not…?'

Lexie swallowed hard, her eyes wide as she watched Lucan cross the kitchen with the slow grace of a jungle cat. 'Why not what?' she prompted distractedly.

'Why not try a pick up line on me?'

Lucan was standing so close now Lexie could feel the warmth of his breath stirring the loose tendrils of hair at her temple as he spoke.

She flicked her tongue nervously across her lips before answering. 'Well, for one thing I make it a rule never to become involved with the people I work for or with.' She had meant the remark to be derisive, but instead she just sounded breathily expectant.

'Is that an old rule or a new one?'

'New. Very new,' Lexie assured him pointedly.

His brows rose speculatively. 'I see…'

'Do you?'

'I believe so,' Lucan murmured softly. 'And does that rule still apply if that employer is only a temporary *temporary* one?'

'Especially then.' She nodded abruptly.

Teasing Lexie had started out as a game to Lucan—a way of prodding at her outspoken and perky self-confidence. It had stopped being a game the moment she'd dismissed any interest in him so arbitrarily.

Lucan hadn't reached the age of thirty-six without knowing when a woman responded to him, and earlier this evening, outside on the steps up to the house, Lexie had been as physically aware of him as Lucan of her. Had been as receptive to his kiss as he to the idea of kissing her...

His gaze dropped to the fullness of her mouth. Those plump and sensuous lips were slightly parted, and still slightly wet from that recent nervous flick of her tongue.

Lucan's breath caught in his throat as she repeated that nervous movement. Her tongue was a moist caress across those parted lips, awakening a hunger in Lucan to do the same...

'Don't!' Lexie gasped, stepping back as she saw Lucan's intention in the raw hunger of his dark gaze. That step brought her up abruptly against one of the kitchen units. 'This is *so* not a good idea, Lucan!' She put her hands up to stop him as he followed her, those hands becoming crushed between them as Lucan leaned his body into hers so that they were now touching from breast to thigh.

Heatedly.

Achingly.

'It feels like a very good idea to me,' Lucan said softly as he moved his arms either side of her, so that his hands could grip the worktop behind her, effectively trapping her as the heat of his body fitted against her much softer curves, his arousal hard against her thighs. 'Doesn't it feel like a good idea to you, Lexie?' he prompted huskily.

Lexie couldn't breathe as she looked up, and instantly felt as if she were drowning in the warmth of those dark and mesmerizing eyes. In the longing she felt to know the touch of Lucan's mouth against her own…

Lucan St Claire's mouth!

Because that was who this man was, Lexie reminded herself desperately. Lucan St Claire. Her beloved Grandpa Alex's eldest son and heir. The same man who, with the rest of his arrogant family, had shunned Lexie's grandmother for so many years.

Ice entered Lexie's veins, and her eyes were glittering with that same cold anger as she straightened. 'Get away from me, Lucan,' she bit out icily, even as she pushed hard against his muscled chest.

Lucan frowned as he easily resisted that push, still holding her captive in the circle of his arms as his hands tightened on the worktop behind her. 'Your lips are saying one thing but your body is saying something else,' he rasped harshly, and he glanced down pointedly at the fullness of her breasts, where the nipples showed hard and aroused against the soft wool of her sweater.

'I'm cold,' she dismissed scornfully. 'Look, Lucan, I'm sure there are plenty of women who would be only too happy to share the bed of the Duke of Stourbridge— temporarily! I just don't happen to be one of them!'

Lucan's eyes narrowed, and he straightened abruptly before stepping away from her. 'I don't remember mentioning that I'm the Duke of Stourbridge.' He eyed her coldly.

She had done it again, Lexie realised sinkingly.

Because she was flustered. Because Lucan was right. Her mouth and her body weren't in agreement at all! Her brain knew that she shouldn't feel this attraction towards Lucan, of all men, but the ache in her body told her it had completely different feelings on the subject.

She breathed raggedly. 'John Barton mentioned it

earlier.' Well…he might have done, mightn't he? 'Imagine my surprise when he referred to you as "His Grace",' she added tauntingly.

'I prefer not to use the title.' Lucan bit the words out as he thrust his hands into his pockets.

'Why not?' Lexie derided. 'Just think of all the extra women you could attract into your bed if they knew you were a duke!'

His eyes narrowed at her obvious mockery. 'I said I prefer not to use it!'

'And I asked why not.'

His mouth thinned to an uncompromising line. 'It's a long story.'

'I'll be happy with the condensed version,' Lexie encouraged huskily.

His nostrils flared angrily. 'There isn't a condensed version.'

'Oh, come on, Lucan—'

'Just leave it alone, will you, Lexie?' he rasped harshly.

Lexie felt a shiver down her spine as she took in the cold glitter of his eyes, the nerve pulsing in his clenched jaw, and the uncompromising—dangerous—set of that sculpted mouth. 'I—okay, fine.' She turned away. 'Perhaps we should eat now?'

Lucan breathed deeply in an effort to control the black tide of anger that had held him in its grip at the reminder of exactly who he was and what he was doing at Mulberry Hall. Most of the time—in fact, all of the time he was in London—Lucan managed to forget completely that the Duke of Stourbridge even existed, let alone had any bearing on his own life.

Because as far as he was concerned it didn't. The title,

Mulberry Hall, the whole damned estate could all just disappear as far as he was concerned.

Damn it, he shouldn't have come back here again so soon after Jordan and Stephanie's wedding. Should have resisted John Barton's suggestion that he come up to Gloucestershire and view the damage for himself.

So why hadn't he…?

Because, Lucan realised with a frown, the idea of being alone for a few days with the beautiful and feisty Lexie Hamilton had somehow appealed to a side of his nature that he was usually at pains to control.

The sensuous side of his nature, which was so much like his father's, and which had caused so much unhappiness to Alexander's wife and sons.

He had decided long ago that no woman would ever lead him around by a certain part of his anatomy. That he would never want, desire *any* woman enough to cause the hurt and destruction that his father had brought on his own family twenty-five years ago, when he'd fallen in love with another woman.

'Lucan…?'

He scowled darkly as he looked up to find that Lexie had placed the casserole in the middle of the table, ready for serving, and was now looking across at him expectantly as she resumed her seat.

He gave a terse shake of his head. 'I don't think I'm hungry after all.'

Lexie gave a pained frown. 'As far as I'm aware, you haven't eaten anything all day…'

Lucan's expression was derisive. 'And that bothers you because…?'

'It doesn't bother me, exactly…'

'That's what I thought,' Lucan drawled ruefully.

She gave an impatient sigh. 'The Bartons didn't even

know I was going to be here, so Cathy Barton obviously prepared this meal for you.'

'Trying to guilt me into eating it, Lexie?' Lucan taunted.

Angry colour entered those ivory cheeks. 'You're being childish now!'

Lucan was usually so emotionally logical—so controlled. Too much so, perhaps? Whatever the reason, he had absolutely no way of stopping the fury that washed over him as he crossed the kitchen in two strides to reach out and pull Lexie effortlessly to her feet and into the prison of his arms. 'Does *this* feel childish to you?' he growled.

Lexie found herself unable to look away from the savagery of Lucan's expression as he loomed over her: hard and glittering dark eyes, clenched cheeks, thinned mouth, that nerve once again pulsing in the firmness of his jaw.

Pulsing with the same rhythm as the hardness of his arousal pressing into the softness of her abdomen…

Whatever she had said or done in the last few minutes, Lexie knew that part of it had somehow pushed Lucan too far—that at this moment he was beyond being reasoned with, beyond denial as his mouth came crushingly down on hers…

He kissed her fiercely, hungrily, tasting, feeding on the softness of her lips. His arms were about her as his hands cupped her bottom and he moulded the heat of her thighs into the hardness of his, lifting her slightly, accommodating her, until he found what he was looking for. Lexie groaned low in her throat as he moved that hardness rhythmically against the apex of her thighs.

She returned that kiss hungrily as she felt herself swell, moisten, felt heat course through her, her breasts becoming full, the nipples hard and aching, as Lucan moved his chest abrasively against her.

Dear Lord, she wanted this man…

Wanted Lucan. Wanted the pleasure she knew he was capable of giving her.

The pleasure he was giving her now as he pushed her sweater up to bare her breasts, before bending his head and drawing one aching nipple hungrily into the heat of his mouth.

Lexie arched her back in invitation, her hands becoming entangled in the dark thickness of Lucan's hair as he suckled her harder, deeper, and his other hand curved possessively over her other breast, to roll the aching nipple between his thumb and finger in rhythmic caress as he suckled its twin.

Lexie felt as if she was on fire. Her skin was intensely sensitised. Hot. Damp. Nothing else mattered at this moment but Lucan and the pleasure—so much pleasure!—he gave her.

She needed to touch him, too. Needed the feel of his bare flesh beneath her hands.

'Oh, God—yes…!' Lucan released Lexie's nipple to groan throatily as he felt her hands on the bareness of his back beneath his sweater. Those small, elegant, sensuous hands moved caressingly across the heat of his back, from the tensed muscles at his shoulders to the low dip of his spine, making him burn, throb, for her to touch him lower still. 'Wrap your legs around me, Lexie!' he instructed fiercely, even as his hands cupped beneath her bottom to lift her fully against his pulsing arousal, and his mouth once again captured hers as he began to thrust slowly, rhythmically, against her.

She was so tiny, so delicately beautiful, and she tasted of honey—warm, hot honey—as Lucan ran his tongue across the sensuous swell of her lips to seek, explore, the moist heat of her mouth.

Her arms were about his neck, her fingers becoming entangled in the hair at his nape as she met the fierce demand of that kiss and the hard demand of his thighs moving against and into hers.

Lucan knew he had never been so aroused. Never been this hard, this aching… Never been so aware of the need to possess, to claim as his own—

No!

Lexie groaned her hunger, her need, as Lucan wrenched his mouth away from hers, steadying her on her own feet before stepping back. That hunger faded, died, and Lexie felt her legs shaking as she looked up to see the angry glitter in the darkness of Lucan's eyes as he glared down at her with fierce intensity.

No—not just fiercely, but almost as if he *hated* her…!

CHAPTER SIX

PERHAPS he did hate her, Lexie realised painfully, as Lucan's already bleak expression turned to one of total disgust, his eyes black and hard as onyx, his top lip curled back almost in a snarl.

Lexie drew in a ragged breath. 'Lucan—'

'You were right. Kissing you was a big mistake!' he rasped scathingly.

Lexie moistened stiff lips. 'I believe what I actually said was that it wasn't a good idea.'

Lucan's mouth thinned. 'Isn't that the same thing?'

'Not at all,' Lexie rallied, as her own anger, her discomfort with the intimacies she had allowed this man, came crashing down on her. He was Lucan St Claire, for God's sake! *Lucan St Claire!* 'I only gave you a cautionary warning—but being told by the man who has just thoroughly kissed you that it was a "big mistake" is damned insulting!'

Lucan looked at Lexie and felt self-disgust begin to fade and irritated amusement take its place as he realised, by the angry sparkle in Lexie's deep blue eyes, the flush to her cheeks and the antagonistic tilt of her stubbornly pointed chin, that she really was insulted by what he had just said.

She wasn't angry because Lucan had kissed her. Or

embarrassed by the fact that her bared breast had been in the heat of his mouth. Nor was she outraged because he had worked his arousal against that swollen and sensitive place between her legs until she groaned and moved against him in her need for release.

Oh, no, it would be too much to expect the unusual, the unique Lexie Hamilton to feel any of those natural reactions to the intimacies they had just shared!

Whereas he—damn it—he was a man who was always in control. Who had always preferred the comfort of a bed when he made love to a woman.

Not with Lexie, apparently. Oh, no. With Lexie he had almost made love in the kitchen at Mulberry Hall. If he hadn't stopped when he had then they would probably have finished making love on the table or the flagstone floor.

Lucan gave a slightly bemused shake of his head as he acknowledged that Lexie was like no other woman he had ever met. Like no woman he had ever *wanted* to meet!

Her long and beautiful black hair had come loose from its plait and now fell in curling and wild disorder about her slender shoulders, and her mouth—that gloriously delicious and sensual mouth—was slightly swollen, the skin beneath slightly reddened from the passion of his kiss.

Lucan's expression darkened as he reached up to gently run the soft pad of his thumb across the mark of that abrasion on her ivory skin. 'I think I need a shave,' he murmured.

Lexie's eyes widened indignantly. This man had just kissed her until she was almost senseless, then insulted her, and all he could say now was— 'Is that it? No apology? No "it won't happen again"? Just "I think I need a shave"!'

He looked down his long, arrogant nose at her. 'I don't feel the need to apologise for something I know you enjoyed as much as I did.' His expression darkened. 'Neither do I believe in making promises I'm not sure I can keep,' he added softly.

Lexie stared at him incredulously for several long seconds before glaring up at him. 'You over-confident, pompous, unmitigated—' She broke off, too angry to be able to come up with a word bad enough to describe his attitude. '*Ass!*' she finally concluded furiously as she stepped away from him.

'Very original,' Lucan drawled dryly.

Lexie's eyes narrowed. 'I doubt you would have appreciated the word I really wanted to use!'

He gave a shake of his head, his expression bleak. 'It can't be any worse than the things I've already called myself.'

She eyed him frustratedly. 'Believe me, if there was some way I could leave here tonight then I would! As there isn't…I'm going upstairs to bed instead.' Lexie grabbed her shoulder-bag from the back of the chair. 'Do you have any preference as to which bedroom I should use? Apart from the ducal suite, of course,' she added scornfully.

'Feel free to use any of them—including the ducal suite,' he added harshly.

'Just because we shared a few kisses, it doesn't mean I'm willing to share your bed—'

'I have no intention, tonight or any other night, of going anywhere near the ducal suite,' he assured her harshly, a nerve pulsing in his tightly clenched jaw. 'With or without you in it.'

Lexie became very still. 'Why not?'

Lucan turned away, the muscles in his back tense. 'Will you stop asking so many damned questions, Lexie, and just go to bed?'

It would be the wise thing to do—the sensible thing to do, when emotions were obviously running so high.

Unfortunately Lexie's actions so far where this particular man was concerned had been neither wise nor sensible.

'You don't use your title. You obviously come here as little as possible. In fact, it's been obvious since John Barton's telephone call this morning that you didn't really want to come here today, either.'

'Is there some point to these observations?' He turned sharply to look at her, those onyx eyes glittering warningly through narrowed lids.

Lexie shrugged. 'It's such a beautiful house—'

'It's a damned mausoleum!' Lucan cut in forcefully.

'Then change it.'

'Changing the décor and the furniture won't make Mulberry Hall somewhere I ever want to live again,' he growled. 'If I could I'd raze the damned place to the ground and grass over it!'

Lexie shook her head. 'I don't understand…'

'You aren't meant to,' Lucan assured her harshly. 'Sharing a few kisses doesn't give you any rights where I'm concerned.'

Lucan never discussed his motives or emotions with anyone—not even with his two brothers. And he was closer to Gideon and Jordan than he was anyone. He certainly didn't intend confiding in Lexie and then having to listen to a lot of amateur psychobabble concerning his lack of ability to deal with his feelings of abandonment after his father left his family for another woman.

'Just go to bed, Lexie,' he advised her dully. 'I'll clear away here.'

Lexie didn't need to be told twice—knew by the bleakness of Lucan's expression that she had already stepped way over the line by probing into things he obviously had no intention of discussing with her.

Which in no way lessened her curiosity concerning Lucan's obvious aversion to Mulberry Hall and all it represented…

'I wondered where you were…'

Lexie turned sharply—guiltily?—to look at Lucan as he strode forcefully down the west gallery to where she stood, looking at the last of the portraits adorning the long gallery wall. A portrait of Alexander St Claire. The fourteenth Duke of Stourbridge.

Lucan's father. Her own beloved Grandpa Alex…

Looking from the portrait to the man who now stood at her side, Lexie could see just how much alike the two men, father and son, actually were.

The portrait of Alexander had obviously been painted when he was about the age Lucan was now. His hair was still black, rather than the iron-grey it had been during the years Lexie had known him, and the similarity of the aristocratic facial structure and dark eyes was unmistakable.

She forced a teasing smile to her lips. 'Did you think I had decided to leave this morning, after all?'

That thought *had* crossed Lucan's mind when he'd gone down to the kitchen and found there was fresh coffee keeping hot in the percolator, and signs of toast having been eaten, but no actual evidence of Lexie herself. It had been pure chance that he had come up to the west gallery, to take another look at the damage before the builder arrived.

Lexie had left her hair loose today, and it framed the delicate beauty of her face before cascading wildly over her shoulders to the middle of her back, appearing very black against the red sweater she wore with faded fitted denims. Denims that clung revealingly to the provocative swell of her bottom—

'Your father?'

Lucan's jaw clenched as he turned his gaze away from that delectable part of Lexie's anatomy to frown up at the portrait of Alexander which Lexie had been studying when he entered the gallery. Unfortunately, it had escaped damage.

'Yes,' he confirmed tightly.

She nodded slowly. 'You're very alike.'

Lucan's mouth thinned. 'Only in looks, I assure you.'

Her head tilted questioningly. 'You don't sound as if you liked your father very much.'

Lucan's eyes narrowed as he looked up again at the painting of Alexander, done forty years ago. It could almost—almost!—have been a portrait of himself.

'I didn't know him well enough to like or dislike him,' he finally bit out coldly.

'I—'

'Lexie, can we talk about something else?' Lucan deliberately turned his back on the portrait of his father and raised a mocking brow as he looked down at her. 'Did you sleep well?'

As it happened, Lexie hadn't slept well at all. Partly because she was so aware of how precarious her position here was. How, at any moment, someone she knew from the village—Cathy Barton, for example—might arrive at Mulberry Hall and recognise her for who and what she was.

But mostly she hadn't been able to sleep because of that incident with Lucan.

Incident? It had been so much more than that.

She had never, ever responded to a man in the wild and wanton way she had to Lucan last night. Never been so aroused, so lost to reason, that nothing else mattered. Not who she was. Not who Lucan was. Certainly not who her grandmother was!

That had come later, as Lexie lay awake in her bed, reliving the sensations aroused by the touch of Lucan's lips and hands. Sensations so soul-deep that she still ached. Still trembled with the memory of that dark head against the paleness of her skin as Lucan suckled and laved her breast with his lips and tongue, the warmth between her thighs. She'd almost felt again the hardness of Lucan's arousal there as he surged rhythmically, pleasurably against her.

And she'd realised that she could no longer deny her attraction to Lucan, nor the desire she felt to make love with him!

She looked now at the way the darkness of his hair fell across his wide brow, at those rock-hewn features that were normally so coldly aristocratic but which she now knew could be flushed and tense with arousal, at the thin chocolate-brown cashmere sweater moulded to the hard-ness of his muscled chest, the faded blue denims doing the same to powerful thighs and long legs. All of those things made Lexie tremble with remembered desire.

Desire for a man who would hate the very air she breathed if he knew she was Sian Thomas's granddaughter!

'I never sleep well the first night in a strange bed,' she dismissed abruptly.

'That must make things a little awkward for you,' he drawled mockingly.

'Not really,' she snapped, knowing exactly what Lucan was implying.

What would Lucan say, do, if she were to tell him that, apart from a few fumbling caresses with the men she had dated in the last couple of years, she had absolutely no physical experience. That the intimacies she had shared with Lucan last night had been completely unprecedented in her life.

'I'm curious as to who these four are?' She moved away to look at a painting on the wall opposite.

Lucan had been totally aware of the way Lexie had been looking at him a few seconds ago. Had seen the hunger in her eyes. The heat. Before she'd shut down both those emotions.

Sensibly.

Wisely.

Lucan accepted it was completely *un*wise on his part, and not in the least sensible, for him to be this physically attracted to Lexie Hamilton—a woman completely unlike the sophisticated women he usually bedded.

Lexie seemed to say the first thing that came into her head, uncaring whether or not it should be said. She probed and poked at emotional wounds Lucan normally discussed with no one. And her responses—those low, keening little cries of pleasure she'd given as Lucan had kissed and caressed her the previous evening—were too raw, too honest. Too addictive…

All of those things were completely dangerous to a man who had never cared enough about any woman to suffer so much as a moment's regret at the ending of one of his always brief relationships…

He wasn't about to suffer one now, over the impulsively outspoken Lexie Hamilton, either!

'The man in the centre of the painting is Hawk, the tenth Duke of Stourbridge, the other three are his siblings— Sebastian, Lucian and Arabella.' Lucan answered her question abruptly.

Her brows rose. 'Is your own name a derivative of Lucian?'

'Probably.' His tone was terse. 'Gideon is a name often used in the family, too.'

Alexander, Lexie knew, was also a St Claire family

name. As well as being Lucan's father's name, it had also been that of his great-great-grandfather.

'I believe,' Lucan continued dismissively, 'the name Gideon came into the family when the Lady Arabella called her first son by that name, in honour of the man who saved her life.'

Lexie's eyes widened. 'How did he do that?'

'I have no idea.' Lucan sounded decidedly uninterested. 'I think we should go back downstairs now; the builder should be arriving at any moment.'

'Of course.' Lexie grimaced as she fell into step beside him, slightly disappointed that Lucan felt disinclined to share the feisty-looking Lady Arabella's story with her. 'Is it okay if I go for a walk in the grounds while you're talking to the builder?' she asked casually.

Deliberately so.

Because she didn't want to alert Lucan to how important the walk was to her. Because a visit to her grandmother's cottage was first on Lexie's list of things to do this morning.

Closely followed by ensuring that Lucan would decide they could go back to London as soon he had spoken to the builder.

After their intimacy yesterday evening Lexie didn't think the two of them spending another night together at Mulberry Hall was a good idea!

'It's going to snow,' Lucan warned her with a frown.

Lexie eyed him teasingly. 'And you know that *how*?'

He looked irritated. 'I know that because I listened to the weather forecast on the radio in the kitchen a few minutes ago!'

'There's no need to get snippy!' she taunted.

'I'm not getting—' Lucan broke off abruptly to draw in a deep, controlling breath. 'You enjoy irritating me, don't you?' he realised frowningly, and easily saw the mischievous glint in Lexie's sparkling blue eyes.

'Love it,' she admitted unrepentantly.

'Because I'm an over-confident, pompous, unmitigated ass?' he came back dryly.

Colour warmed her cheeks at this reminder of the names she had called him the night before. She grimaced. 'You remember every word...'

'Well, of course I remember every word!' Lucan chuckled softly. 'Of their kind, they were unique.'

She frowned up at him. 'In what way?'

'In every way.' Lucan still smiled.

Lexie gave a self-conscious wince. 'Meaning that no one has ever spoken to you in that way before?'

'Meaning that no one has ever spoken to me in that way before,' he continued mockingly.

She grimaced. 'Oh, dear.'

Lucan found himself chuckling again. He couldn't seem to help himself when confronted with Lexie's blunt honesty. 'You could try looking a little less pleased with yourself!'

She raised dark brows. 'What would be the point, when that's exactly how I feel?'

He gave a rueful shake of his head and stood back to allow Lexie to precede him into the warmth of the kitchen. 'Do you always say the first thing that comes into your head?'

Lexie nodded. 'Usually.' But not always, she acknowledged with a frown. And she definitely needed to practise caution when in the company of this particular man.

Something she was finding she liked doing less and less...

It had been fun to tease Lucan just now, to see and hear

him laugh, to forget for a few minutes who he was and who she was.

Dear Lord—she couldn't actually be interested in a *relationship* with Lucan, could she…?

She had done some pretty stupid things in her time—deciding to stand in as Lucan's PA for three days being only one of them—but to allow this attraction she felt for him, the undeniable hunger she felt for more of Lucan's kisses and caresses to continue, would be sheer madness on her part.

A madness that wasn't going to happen!

She turned to look up at him challengingly. 'For instance, at this moment I want to say I really need to get out of this stuffy atmosphere and into the fresh air!'

Lucan's eyes narrowed as he returned the challenge in Lexie's gaze. 'Is it the house you find stuffy, or me…?'

'I'll leave that for you to decide!' she came back perkily, before grabbing her coat from the back of the chair and letting herself out, without giving Lucan the chance to reply.

Not that Lucan would have done so in any case. He had never run after a woman in his life, and he wasn't about to start now.

Even if part of him wanted to…

Lexie took a snow-covered path through the woods at the back of Mulberry Hall to her grandmother's cottage, situated on the very edge of the village. A path that in the past had been well-worn by Alexander St Claire, during the years he had visited the woman he loved.

Her grandmother's cottage looked the same as it always had as Lexie stepped out into a clearing at the back of the small white-painted building. The windows gleamed brightly, and the thatch on the roof looked new when she glanced up and saw the inviting curl of smoke drifting delicately from the chimney.

Lexie drew in a deep breath as she hesitated outside the red-painted front door of the cottage, knowing she would have some explaining to do once she was inside.

And also knowing that what had happened last night between herself and Lucan, this attraction for him that Lexie was trying so desperately to fight, wouldn't be a part of the conversation…!

CHAPTER SEVEN

'WHERE the hell have you been?' Lucan demanded furiously.

Lexie had paused in the kitchen doorway to brush the snow from her hair and coat. She glanced across the kitchen as a chair scraped on the flagstones and he stood up from his seat at the oak table, his expression grim.

'Sorry…?' she said lightly as she carefully closed the kitchen door behind her.

Lucan wasn't fooled for a moment by the innocence of her expression. 'You gave me the impression you were only going for a stroll in the grounds, and you've been gone for over two hours!' he bit out coldly.

She raised dark brows. 'Did you have some work you wanted me to do?'

'Obviously not, when I've been talking to the builder.'

'Then I don't understand the problem…?'

'The problem is that it began to snow not long after you left the house,' he said, with a pointed glance at the dampness caused by the snow melting in Lexie's hair.

'Surely you weren't *worried* about me, Lucan?' she taunted dryly.

As it happened, yes, Lucan *had* been concerned by Lexie's prolonged absence. Not only was it freezing cold outside, but the predicted snow had started to fall heavily almost as soon as Lexie had stepped out of the house, and was now a couple of inches deep on the ground.

'It isn't a question of being worried, Lexie,' he dismissed impatiently. 'You aren't familiar with the area,' he continued tautly. 'You could have fallen through the ice on the lake and drowned, for all I knew.'

'You aren't thinking positively, Lucan. At least that way I wouldn't be here annoying you any more,' she said ruefully as she slipped her damp coat down her arms to drape it across the back of one of the chairs to dry.

Lucan felt an icy chill down his spine as he immediately had an image of Lexie's dead body floating beneath the layer of ice that presently covered the lake behind Mulberry Hall.

'Damn it, this isn't funny, Lexie!'

'It wasn't meant to be.' She snapped her own impatience with the conversation. 'And I'm no more used to answering to anyone for my actions than *you* are,' she added pointedly.

'While you're staying here with me you had better get used to it!' Lucan grated harshly.

She became very still. 'I think not,' she returned evenly, the angry glitter of her eyes a complete contradiction to that vocal calmness.

It was a warning Lucan had no intention of heeding.

He hadn't been too worried when it first began to snow—had believed those icy flakes would bring Lexie back to the house sooner rather than later. When the minutes had ticked past, passing an hour, he had put on his own coat in order to go outside and look for her.

Unfortunately, the grounds of Mulberry Hall were vast—too much for Lucan to be able to search them properly. He hadn't even been able to find any footprints in the snow to tell him which direction Lexie might have taken on her walk. After twenty minutes of futile searching he had returned to the kitchen to sit and wait for her.

His temper rising by the minute.

Which—considering Lucan hadn't even realised he *had* a temper until he'd met Lexie Hamilton—didn't bode well for the outcome of their present conversation.

'I think *yes,*' he ground out harshly.

Her mouth firmed. 'You can think what you damn well please, Lucan, but that isn't going to make it happen.'

'Where were you for the last two hours?' Lucan's voice was hard as he reverted to his original question.

A question Lexie had no intention of answering honestly.

Because she couldn't.

Her grandmother had been surprised but overjoyed to see Lexie again so soon after spending the Christmas holiday in London with all the family. Less pleased once she'd realised how and why Lexie was here…

It hadn't been a comfortable conversation. Her grandmother was totally disapproving of Lexie's subterfuge in going to work for Lucan in the first place. And deeply concerned at the way it had backfired on Lexie so that she'd had no choice but to accompany Lucan to Mulberry Hall yesterday.

Her grandmother had given dire warning as to Lucan's reaction if he should discover the truth.

A totally unnecessary warning; Lexie already knew how angry Lucan was going to be if he ever learnt she was Sian Thomas's granddaughter. How much he was going to hate himself—and her—for having kissed her…

Her gaze avoided meeting his probing dark one. 'I told you—I was walking.'

'Walking where?' Lucan studied her through narrowed lids, having noted that evasion and wondering at the reason for it. As far as he was aware Lexie had never been to Gloucestershire before, didn't know anyone in the area—so what was her problem with telling him where she had been?

'Here and there.' She kept her tone light as she moved to pour herself a mug of coffee. 'Want some?' She held up the coffee pot invitingly.

'No.' Lucan was still far from satisfied with her answer. 'What I want is to know where you've been all this time.'

'For God's sake, Lucan. I'm a grown woman, not a child!' She slammed the coffee pot back down on the percolator before turning to glare at him.

Lucan's mouth firmed as he strode forcefully across the kitchen until he stood directly in front of Lexie, effectively blocking her exit if she should try to make one. 'Neither you nor your coat appear to be particularly wet, so you obviously took shelter somewhere—'

'And you obviously missed your vocation as a nosy busybody!' she cut in mockingly.

Lucan drew in a harshly controlling breath, hands clenched at his sides as he glared down at her. 'You are the most infuriating, impossible, stubborn woman I have ever had the misfortune to meet.'

She grimaced. 'Which makes me more than a match for an over-confident, pompous ass, wouldn't you say?'

She had done it again, Lucan realised as he felt his anger begin to evaporate and amusement take its place. The tension began to ease from his shoulders as he gave a derisive smile. 'You really *are* impossible, you know.'

'I *do* know, actually.' She nodded ruefully. 'From all accounts I used to drive my parents to distraction when I was younger. It's probably the reason I'm an only child!'

Lucan realised it was the first real piece of personal

information she had given him. 'What's that like? I grew up with two brothers only two years younger than I am, so I can't imagine what it must be like to be an only child.'

'It could be a little lonely on occasion,' Lexie admitted cautiously, having no intention of telling him any more details about herself. 'But obviously I survived the hardship,' she dismissed brightly as she straightened. 'So, what are we going to do for the rest of the day? Do you want to do some of the work you brought with you? Or should we try to drive back to London now, before the snow gets any deeper?' she added, with a frown looking out of the kitchen window at the steadily falling snow.

She certainly didn't want to get snowed in at Mulberry Hall for several days—and nights—with Lucan!

'Just think, Lucan,' she added encouragingly. 'I could be out of your hair in just a matter of hours!'

It *would* be a good idea to try and get back to London today, Lucan inwardly acknowledged as he frowned. And not only because of the snow!

Staying on here for another day or so with Lexie—a woman who succeeded in making him laugh when it was the last thing he wanted to do—could be a mistake on his part. A big mistake.

And yet...

Therein lay the problem.

After years of avoiding coming anywhere near the Mulberry Hall estate, and all it represented, a part of Lucan was now reluctant to leave. Not because he wanted to be at Mulberry Hall itself, but because he was pretty sure that Lexie, once back in London, would make sure the agency she worked for immediately replaced her as his PA.

But wasn't that what Lucan had decided he wanted last night, after Lexie had left the kitchen to go to bed? To put her out of his life? To never see or hear from her again? To once again put himself behind that barrier of cold aloofness that he allowed no one to penetrate?

That was exactly what he had decided!

And yet...

'You seem to be taking an awful long time to decide, Lucan.' Lexie broke teasingly into his thoughts.

He looked down into her upturned face. 'Much as I might want to return to London, I'm not willing to do it at the risk of either your safety or my own. That being the case, we'll give it a couple of hours and see if the snow stops.'

One dark brow quirked. 'And if it gets worse instead...?'

He shrugged. 'Then I guess we're stuck with each other for another night.'

Which was exactly what Lexie *didn't* want.

What she had assured her grandmother wouldn't happen!

Nanna Sian had been as concerned for Lexie as she was for Lucan St Claire. Her grandmother knew only too well how much the St Claire family hated her, and consequently anyone connected to her. The only thing that had soothed her grandmother's anxiety was Lexie giving her word that she would put an end to this situation as soon as she and Lucan returned to London.

Unfortunately, when Lexie had made that promise she hadn't taken into account the possibility of being snowed in here with Lucan for several days!

She gave a firm shake of her head. 'I think we should leave now.'

Lucan eyed Lexie mockingly as he took in the wilful sparkle in her eyes and the stubborn set to her mouth. 'In case you haven't realised it yet, Lexie, this is a dictatorship, not a democracy! And, as the driver of the only vehicle at our disposal, I have decided that the conditions aren't safe for us to leave yet.'

A frown appeared between those dark brows. 'Isn't it just for conditions like this that you *have* a four-wheel drive vehicle, for goodness' sake!'

He shrugged. 'I'm still not willing to take the risk. That being the case, what's for lunch?' he added tauntingly.

She frowned up at him. 'As you're obviously the dictator, and I'm only the poor, oppressed peasant, I suggest *you* decide. And once you've decided I suggest that you also prepare it. I am going upstairs to pack my bag, ready for when we can leave!' She turned on her heel and marched out of the kitchen.

Lucan gave a wolfish grin as he stood and enjoyed watching the provocative sway of Lexie's denim-clad hips and perfectly rounded bottom until she had left the room and slammed the kitchen door behind her.

Lexie Hamilton might be infuriating and impossible, and stubborn as a mule, but she was also the sexiest bundle of femininity Lucan had ever met.

Dangerously so…

'Well?'

Lucan relaxed back in his chair to look across at Lexie as she appeared in the kitchen doorway. 'Well, what?'

Lexie eyed him frustratedly as he continued to sit calmly at the kitchen table, eating toast. 'In case you haven't noticed, it's stopped snowing.' There was only a couple of inches of snow on the ground outside, which certainly wasn't enough to hamper the progress of the monster vehicle parked outside in the driveway.

'I noticed.'

'Well?'

'W—'

'If you say "well, what?" again I may be provoked into hitting you!' Lexie warned between gritted teeth, breathing hard in the face of Lucan's unruffled calm when she was so agitated she really could have hit something. Or someone!

The visit to her grandmother earlier had only emphasised how vulnerable Lexie was—how at any minute she could be exposed as the granddaughter of Sian Thomas.

And if that happened then not only would Lucan make Lexie personally suffer for that exposure, but probably Premier Personnel, too…

Lucan raised dark brows. 'I was actually going to ask what's in London for you to rush back to?'

'Civilisation?' she came back scathingly.

Once again Lucan found himself laughing at one of Lexie's remarks. At the way she didn't even attempt to stop herself from saying the first thing that came into her head. It was totally refreshing to a man who always thought long and hard before speaking. Mainly because millions of pounds and thousands of people's jobs very often depended upon what Lucan did or didn't say, but also because that was just the way he was. The way he had deliberately schooled himself to be.

He gave a rueful shake of his head. 'It will still be there tomorrow.'

'I want to go back *today*!'

Lucan shrugged. '"I want" doesn't always get.'

'You're being ridiculous again—'

'No, Lexie, I think at the moment *you* have the monopoly on that,' he said harshly.

'I'm not the one who's being so difficult about leaving.'

'John mentioned before he left yesterday that there are

some things he needs to discuss with me before I go back to London.' Lucan frowned down at her.

Lexie stilled. 'Estate business?'

'I believe so, yes.' Lucan gave a slow inclination of his head.

'Oh.' Lexie felt like a deflated balloon at the realisation that Lucan wasn't just being bloody-minded, after all. He had a perfectly valid reason for staying on awhile longer.

Why had Lucan had to laugh again in that totally unself-conscious way?

It changed his whole appearance—gave warmth to the darkness of his eyes, revealed laughter lines beside that sculpted mouth, as well as that cleft in his left cheek. A very sexy cleft. A sexy cleft that made Lexie want to move closer and lick it, taste it with her tongue—

Oh, good Lord!

Why did just being anywhere near this man now make her think about sex?

About having sex.

No, not sex. Making love. Sex for sex's sake had never appealed to Lexie. Which was probably why she was still a virgin at twenty-four!

Even so, Lexie had absolutely no doubt that the person she wanted to make love to and with was definitely Lucan. *Only* Lucan.

Was this the same emotional and physical trap that her grandmother had fallen into all those years ago when she'd first met Alexander? Did Lucan, as far as Lexie was concerned, possess the same magnetic hold over her that his father had held over Sian? The sort of magnetic hold that could reduce a woman who was usually sensible, logical, into forgetting everything else but him?

If he did, then Lexie wanted no part of it!

'If it's estate business…' She nodded abruptly, very conscious of how close Lucan was standing to her.

'That's very understanding of you,' he murmured huskily.

'I think so.' Lexie couldn't look away from those mesmerising dark eyes. Could feel the heat emanating from her own body now as well as Lucan's. A heat that doubled, tripled, when Lucan raised one of his hands and curved it over the warm contours of her cheek. 'What are you doing?' she breathed unevenly.

He gave a half-smile. 'You're looking a little… flushed.'

Lexie was more than a little flushed—and not just outwardly. She felt that familiar fire once again burning between her thighs.

Lucan raised one dark brow. 'You aren't coming down with something, are you?'

Lucanitis, probably!

Lexie had to say something, do something—anything to break this magnetic pull that just made her want to move closer to the warmth of this man's body. 'Do you always wear your hair so short…?'

He frowned slightly and raised his other hand to run it through that dark hair. 'You don't approve?' His voice was gravelly and low.

Lexie looked up at him consideringly. 'It makes you look…'

'Older?' he suggested harshly.

'I was going to say severe,' she corrected dryly.

He gave a mocking half smile. 'But I *am* severe, Lexie.'

Not all the time. Most definitely not all the time!

In fact, standing this close to him, with the heat from their bodies mingling, matching, Lexie was finding it harder and harder to think of him as the arrogant and aloof Lucan St Claire!

Which wasn't surprising when what she most wanted to do at that moment was rip those faded denims and that brown sweater from the muscled leanness of Lucan's body and caress and taste every inch of him!

Help…!

Lexie definitely needed help. Something to give her the strength, the will, to fight this growing attraction she felt for Lucan.

Where was a lightning bolt when she most needed one?

Lucan was totally aware of the tension that permeated the room. A sexual, sensual tension that swirled around the two of them like an ever-deepening, sense-drugging transparent mist.

He looked down into the deep, dark blue of Lexie's eyes before moving his gaze lower, to the soft pout of her lips. Plump and enticing lips, which parted slightly even as he looked at them. As if knowing, waiting for his kiss.

The skin of Lexie's cheek felt like velvet against the palm of his hand, reminding him all too forcefully of how her bared breasts had felt as velvety soft as he'd cupped them the previous evening, before caressing and savouring them with his hands and mouth. Inciting a need deep inside him to touch and taste her like that again…

'Lexie—' He broke off as a knock sounded briefly on the outside door before it was pushed open and John Barton stood framed in the doorway.

The caretaker shivered in the icy wind blowing outside and stepped quickly into the room to close the door behind him. Coming to an abrupt halt, he glanced across the kitchen to where Lucan and Lexie stood so close together they were almost touching…

CHAPTER EIGHT

'I'M NOT interrupting anything, am I?' John Barton continued to hesitate near the door.

Not interrupting anything…!

Lexie didn't even want to think about what John Barton had so nearly interrupted as she shifted sideways and then stepped completely away from the heat and seduction of Lucan's body so close to her own.

Once across the kitchen she was at least able to breathe more easily—even managing to give a strained smile to the obviously uncomfortable, but also slightly curious, John Barton.

'Has it started snowing again…?' She gave a dismayed frown as she saw the droplets of moisture on his sandy-coloured hair.

'I'm afraid so.' He shrugged, with another awkward glance in Lucan's direction.

Lucan straightened abruptly, only the glittering black onyx of his eyes revealing—to Lexie, at least—his displeasure at the other man's untimely interruption.

Or perhaps that displeasure was levelled at Lexie?

His firmly clenched jaw and those cold dark eyes, as he turned to look directly at her, certainly didn't give the impression that she had escaped Lucan's displeasure. A fact that instantly raised Lexie's hackles.

Damn it, she wasn't the one who had initiated the intimacy between them. The one who had tried to seduce her with a touch. Who would have kissed her—probably more than kissed her—if John Barton hadn't interrupted them!

'I suggest we go to my study and talk, John,' Lucan stated coldly as he saw the angry sparkle building in Lexie's expressive eyes. 'Lexie informs me she wants to get back to London as soon as possible,' he added, having noted the look of dismay on Lexie's face when she had realised it was snowing again, and the possibility of delaying their departure. Something she obviously wasn't too happy about.

Lucan couldn't say he was exactly happy at the thought of staying on here with Lexie any longer, either.

He had thought when he'd insisted on bringing her here that she would be a diversion—a way for him to be at Mulberry Hall without his usual feelings of aversion. Instead, Lexie had made him forget all caution, all those barriers Lucan had so carefully placed about his emotions over the years. To the point where all he could think about now was touching her again, kissing her, making love to her.

If John hadn't arrived when he had—

'I merely commented that if we didn't want to get snowed in then we should probably leave sometime today.' She looked across at him challengingly.

Lucan glanced out of the window. He could see that the snow was falling heavily again. 'I think it may already be too late for that…'

Lexie glanced out of the kitchen window, too, her heart sinking as she saw the huge flakes of snow falling delicately past the window. Her eyes narrowed accusingly as she turned back to Lucan. 'If we had left when I first suggested it—'

'Then we would be out in the middle of it right now,' Lucan reasoned impatiently. 'I have no doubt that the motorways will have been kept clear, but I very much doubt the small country roads we'd have to travel on first will have received the same treatment.'

He was right, of course, Lexie acknowledged heavily. As usual.

She straightened. 'I'll leave the two of you to have your talk—'

'You need to eat some lunch first,' Lucan cut in firmly.

Lexie's cheeks warmed at having John Barton witness this exchange. 'I'm really not hungry—'

'You need to stay here and eat,' Lucan insisted.

What Lexie needed and what she wanted were two entirely different things.

She might possibly need to eat something, but what she wanted was to get as far away from Lucan as it was possible for her to be. But, as Lucan had already pointed out to her once today, 'I want' didn't always get…

'Fine,' she managed tautly, hoping that Lucan had picked up on her tone, and the warning in the glance she gave him. Otherwise—John Barton's presence or not—she was going to be forced into saying something they might all regret.

The younger man gave her a rueful smile. 'Cathy's longing to come over and say hello.'

'Oh?' Lexie felt flustered at the mere idea of John's wife coming to the house. It might not be the Cathy she knew, but chances were—the way Lexie's luck was going—that she was.

John nodded. 'But I didn't think it was a good idea for her to come over today, in this weather. She's expecting our first baby in three months' time,' he explained happily.

'Congratulations! Maybe next time.' Lexie managed to

gather herself enough to speak, knowing there wouldn't be a 'next time' at Mulberry Hall for her. Not if she had any say in the matter. And she did.

Lucan gave her one last questioning glance through narrowed lids before he and John went out into the hallway.

Alerting Lexie to the fact that she hadn't quite managed to hide the panic she'd felt when John had told her Cathy wanted to come over and say hello…

'So what's your problem with meeting Cathy Barton?' Lucan prompted as soon as he rejoined Lexie in the kitchen once John had left.

'Sorry?' Lexie raised innocent brows as she turned from staring accusingly out of the window at the falling snow.

To Lucan's sharp gaze Lexie's expression looked a little too innocent to be true. 'You seemed…unsettled earlier by the idea of meeting Cathy Barton.'

'Don't be silly, Lucan,' she dismissed lightly. 'If I appeared concerned then it was probably at the thought of a heavily pregnant woman even thinking of venturing outside in this weather.'

Except Lucan knew that John hadn't mentioned that his wife was pregnant until *after* Lexie had responded so alarmingly to his statement that Cathy wanted to meet Lexie…

'Your concern is admirable,' he drawled dryly. 'So you don't have any objections to meeting her?'

'I've just said that I don't,' Lexie answered slowly, warily, not at all happy with the challenge she sensed in Lucan's attitude.

He nodded. 'In that case there's no problem with my having accepted the Bartons' invitation for both of us to join them for dinner this evening.'

Lexie's only outward show of emotion at that statement

was the curling of her hands into fists at her sides. Hands that clenched so tightly her nails were digging painfully into her palms.

Have dinner with the Bartons? With Cathy Barton—a woman Lexie was becoming more and more convinced was the Cathy Wilson she had known and been friends with all those years ago.

She swallowed hard. 'Is it a good idea for us to go out in this weather?'

Lucan gave a rueful shrug. 'I think we're going to have to if we want to eat something other than toast.' He gave a pointed glance at the empty plate in front of Lexie, with several toast crumbs still on its surface.

'We still have Cathy's casserole from last night,' Lexie reminded him.

He grimaced. 'I doubt that's going to be very appetising when it's already been warmed up once and left.'

Lexie was starting to feel more and more as if she were standing in quicksand rather than snow.

'We could always go to the pub in the village, I suppose,' Lucan continued lightly. 'Although that might be a little insulting when I've already accepted John's invitation.' He quirked dark questioning brows.

'Why don't *you* go?' Lexie encouraged, her voice brittle. 'I'm not really hungry after eating toast, and I'm feeling a little tired, too, after my walk this morning. I'll probably just read for a bit and then have an early night.'

'An early night sounds good.'

It also, Lexie thought warily, sounded slightly threatening when Lucan said it in that sensually husky voice.

She looked at him searchingly, sure she saw a glint of laughter lurking in the darkness of his eyes before it was quickly masked. Could he possibly be playing with her? If he was, then he had chosen the wrong woman to play with!

'You *have* to go to the Bartons, Lucan,' she insisted. 'It would look rude if neither of us showed up after you've accepted the invitation.'

He shrugged. 'I've never had a problem in the past with people thinking I'm rude.'

'I can personally vouch for that,' Lexie muttered disgustedly.

'And it isn't a problem for me now, either,' Lucan continued dryly. 'But if it bothers you…'

'It doesn't,' she assured him quickly.

'Then I'll telephone and make our excuses.'

She gave an impatient shake of her head. 'That isn't very fair, when Cathy has probably already started cooking for you.'

'For *us*,' he corrected pointedly.

'You're the one that's important,' Lexie reasoned derisively. 'After all, I'm just an insignificant PA—a temporary one at that. Whereas you're the local celebrity. The illustrious Duke of Stourbridge,' she added tauntingly.

He gave a rueful shake of his head. 'Temporary PA or otherwise, there's nothing in the least insignificant about *you*, Lexie,' he said dryly.

'You know exactly what I meant!' she snapped impatiently.

Yes, Lucan knew exactly what Lexie was up to…

'Neither is there anything in the least illustrious about the title of Duke of Stourbridge!' he added bitterly.

'Oh?'

'*Oh*,' he echoed unhelpfully, having no intention of satisfying her obvious curiosity by opening up that particular can of worms. 'As I've already told you, the title doesn't interest me.'

'Whether you choose to use the title or not, that's obviously how the people of Stourbridge think of you,' she came back dismissively.

Lucan's eyes narrowed. 'And how would *you* know how the people of Stourbridge think of me…?'

Yet another slip, Lexie realised with a self-disgusted wince. She really wasn't very good at this.

Damn it—it was a little late for her to realise that she should have just refused to come here and invited Lucan to do his worst where Premier Personnel was concerned!

'It's pretty obvious that John Barton is slightly in awe of you.' She shrugged. 'Besides, all small villages function on gossip, don't they?'

'Do they?'

'Oh, stop being difficult, Lucan! If you had bothered to consult me before accepting John's invitation then you would have known that I'm not in the mood to play lowly servant to your arrogant duke in public!'

Lucan's eyes narrowed on Lexie as he drew in a long, slow, calming breath, knowing that by referring to his title again she was deliberately trying to annoy him. He had no intention of giving her that satisfaction.

He knew that something was slightly off about Lexie's behaviour. Something he couldn't quite put his finger on but nevertheless could sense was there.

Perhaps it was her avoidance of telling him where she had gone on her walk this morning? Or her reluctance to go to the Bartons' for dinner? Or perhaps the fact that she'd seemed just as reluctant to eat at the pub in the village, both last night and again today?

At the moment, all Lucan was sure of was that there had been something different about Lexie's behaviour, something guarded, since they'd arrived at Mulberry Hall yesterday…

He regarded her consideringly. 'What *are* you in the mood for?'

Lexie gave a start even as she eyed him warily. 'I told you—an early night.'

Lucan shrugged. 'And I've already agreed that sounds like a good idea.'

As far as Lexie could tell Lucan hadn't moved from his stance near the cooker, and yet she still found herself taking a defensive step backwards. Away from him. Away from the danger Lucan suddenly represented. The physical danger…

Her tongue moved nervously, moistly, across her suddenly dry lips. 'I have no idea what your usual arrangement is with your PA, Lucan, but I can assure you—'

'Oh, I think my "usual arrangement" with my PA has been made more than obvious by the fact that the last one walked out on me before Christmas, without giving notice, and that I didn't even get her name right yesterday,' Lucan drawled. 'Don't you?' he added challengingly.

Yes, Lexie was more convinced than ever that part of the reason—the *main* reason—Jessica Brown had left her employment at the St Claire Corporation was because she hadn't succeeded in tempting Lucan into a personal relationship with her.

So why did Lexie suddenly feel that without even trying the opposite was true where she was concerned? That if she gave Lucan the slightest encouragement she would be in his arms. In his bed.

Maybe it was the heat she could now see in Lucan's coal-black eyes as they swept over her slowly from her toes to the top of her head? Or the sensual softening of that sculpted mouth? Or perhaps it was the fact that he was once again standing much too close to her, the heat in his dark gaze intensifying as it shifted to her mouth…

How could she not have noticed, been aware of the soft, panther-like tread that had brought Lucan across the kitchen so that once again he stood only inches away from her?

This time Lexie had nowhere to go. She was already backed up against one of the kitchen cabinets. Her eyes were wide as she looked up at Lucan, her throat moving convulsively as she swallowed before speaking. 'Look, I realise this is the warmest room in the house, but even so I don't think that gives you the right to try and make love to me every time we're alone in here together.'

'*Try* and make love to you, Lexie?' he drawled softly.

Her cheeks felt warm. 'Don't you have some sort of un-written policy concerning not getting personally involved with your employees?'

He gave a derisive smile. 'I think it's a little late to worry about that in our particular case, don't you?'

Because this man had already kissed Lexie, caressed her, touched her more intimately than any other man ever had in all of her twenty-four years!

'Besides,' Lucan continued dryly, 'you and I both know that you have no intention of still being my employee once we get back to London.'

'Do we?'

His smile widened, revealing even white teeth against those sensually carved lips. 'Oh, yes,' he acknowledged softly. 'Which means there's absolutely no reason why we can't…pursue a relationship now.'

'Pursue a relationship…?' Lexie repeated inanely. And was that high-pitched squeak *really* her voice? She sounded like Minnie Mouse on helium!

Lucan frowned his impatience with what he was sure was Lexie being deliberately obtuse. She knew—couldn't help but know—of the physical awareness between the two of them. Of the way the very air seemed to sizzle with that awareness whenever the two of them were alone together.

Having decided last night, and again earlier, that he couldn't allow Lexie into his life, Lucan had then spent the hour in the study with John Barton thinking of her rather than listening to anything the other man said. Most of all of how his body hardened in arousal every time he was anywhere near her...

The sensible thing to do would be to continue fighting that attraction until they were back in London and Lexie had gone out of his life.

The fact that he hadn't heard a single word John had said to him during that hour told Lucan that it was already too late for that. He needed to get Lexie out of his system now. And the only way he could think of to do that was to take their relationship to the next level.

Invariably once the chase was over and he'd had sex with a woman—any woman—Lucan completely lost interest. Lexie wasn't—couldn't be—any different. Besides, he had never been a man who ran away from his problems. And Lexie was becoming more and more of a problem with every minute spent with her.

'Oh, come on, Lexie,' he chided huskily. 'We're both adults. We know exactly what's going on here—'

'*Nothing* is going on here!' she cut in determinedly. 'Now, would you please step away from me?' Her hands rose to push against his chest.

Lucan immediately felt the warmth of those hands through his thin cashmere sweater. Such tiny, elegant hands. Hands that he wanted to feel on every inch of his flesh. Every aroused inch!

His gaze easily held hers as his hands moved up and over hers, pressing their warmth against him, making Lexie totally aware of the beating of his heart as it throbbed in rhythm with his pulsing arousal. That same heat had caused Lexie's eyes to brighten feverishly and her cheeks to flush.

'Do you still think nothing is going on here, Lexie?' Lucan prompted huskily.

Of *course* Lexie knew that something was going on between the two of them; she might be physically inexperienced, but she wasn't stupid. She knew that there had been something between the two of them from the moment they'd first met. The problem was Lexie had thought it was dislike, when in reality it was the opposite. At least definitely desire...

The look of determination in Lucan's eyes told her that he wanted to take that *something* a step further.

She gave a shake of her head. 'I'm not into having casual affairs with my boss.'

'It doesn't have to be that casual,' he assured her huskily.

'What?' Lexie's heart was beating so fast, so loudly, that she was sure Lucan couldn't help but be aware of it. Or of the heat, the scent of her arousal emanating from her body in heady waves...

Lucan shrugged. 'Instead of going back to London, maybe meeting up there occasionally, we could stay on here for several more days and see the whole thing through.'

Lexie eyed him disbelievingly. 'To its bitter end, no doubt?'

His smile was rueful as he shook his head. 'It doesn't have to be that way.'

'Believe me, between us it would be.' Lexie had good reason for knowing it would.

'You don't know that—'

'How long do your affairs usually last, Lucan? A couple

of weeks? A month? And then what? A nice piece of expensive and ostentatious jewellery as payment for services rendered? A costly gesture to ensure there are no hurt feelings?' Her mouth twisted scornfully.

Lucan's jaw tightened. 'My women don't usually leave with hurt feelings.'

'No, they leave with that expensive piece of jewellery!' Lexie gave an inelegant snort. 'I very much doubt that I'm your usual type of woman, Lucan!'

No, she wasn't, Lucan acknowledged impatiently. Which was why he had decided the best thing to do was to stay on here and get this inexplicable desire he felt for her out of his system.

He should have known it wouldn't be that easy. This was Lexie, for goodness' sake. The most frustrating woman— on so many levels—that he had ever had the misfortune to meet.

A woman whose only pieces of jewellery were pearl earrings and that simple gold locket she habitually wore about her slender neck...

Lucan's eyes narrowed on that gold oval where it nestled against her breasts. 'Whose picture do you have in the locket, Lexie?'

'What...?' She looked panicked as Lucan moved one of his hands up to cradle the gold locket in his palm. 'Don't touch that!' She slapped at that hand.

Lucan's fingers instantly closed about the locket, his eyes glittering darkly as he saw that the colour had drained from Lexie's face, leaving her cheeks pale and her eyes dark and haunted. 'Who is it, Lexie?' he repeated harshly. 'Some long lost lover you still pine for? Or someone you have in your life now? Someone whose picture you carry around next to your heart?' he added.

'And what if it is?' Lexie tried unsuccessfully to release

the locket from his closed fingers. 'I said let *go*, Lucan,' she grated between clenched teeth.

'Make me,' he challenged softly.

Lexie tried, but Lucan's fingers were closed about the locket like a steel trap, just as impenetrable. So much so that after several seconds of struggle the chain on the locket suddenly broke.

Lexie stared down disbelievingly at the broken chain as it dangled loosely over those lean but powerful fingers.

The antique gold locket and chain had been a sixteenth birthday gift from Nanna Sian and Grandpa Alex—the last they had ever given her together. Grandpa Alex had died only weeks later. And inside, together for ever, were smiling photographs of them both.

CHAPTER NINE

'No!' LEXIE choked. 'What have you *done*?'

What the hell had he been thinking? Lucan questioned self-disgustedly as he saw tears balancing on Lexie's lashes as she stared down, disbelieving, at the broken chain, at the locket still firmly clasped in the palm of Lucan's hand.

The simple truth was he hadn't been thinking at all—only reacting. In a way he could never remember reacting before as he'd become lost in a rising black tide of—

Of what?

Lucan felt stunned by his actions and shied away from answering that question.

'I'm sorry, Lexie—'

'Sorry?' she repeated, her voice high. 'Sorry?' she repeated disbelievingly. 'You behave like a complete Neanderthal a few minutes ago, succeeding in breaking my necklace in the process, and all you can do is say you're sorry?' She gave an emotional shake of her head. 'Give that to me!' She snatched the locket out of Lucan's hand the moment he relaxed his grip on it.

'I'll buy you a new chain as soon as—'

'I don't want a new chain!' Her eyes flashed in warning as she glared up at him.

'Then I'll have that one repaired—'

'I'll get it repaired myself, thank you very much,' she ground out icily.

Lucan hadn't missed the way Lexie's own fingers had tightened about the locket now. Protectively? Lovingly...? 'I'm responsible for breaking it, so I should—'

'You've already done enough, Lucan,' she assured him flatly. 'Now, I am going upstairs to my room, to read for a while before I go to bed, and you—you can do what the hell you please!'

Those tears on Lexie's lashes were in complete contrast to the aggression of her words. Not that Lucan didn't fully deserve her anger. He had behaved like an idiot a few minutes ago. An unthinking, mindless—what? Lexie had called him a Neanderthal, but what had he *really* been thinking, feeling, when he'd demanded to know whose photograph she carried in her locket?

Damn it—no wonder Lucan hadn't immediately recognised the emotion for what it was! How could he, when it was an emotion he had never experienced before?

Jealousy.

Pure, unadulterated, green-eyed, monstrous jealousy.

An emotion Lucan had always considered completely irrational. Certainly not one he had ever felt over any woman before.

And yet he was aware that he still felt it. Those tears glistening on Lexie's lashes seemed to confirm that the locket did indeed contain a photograph of someone she'd loved. Was possibly still in love with.

So what? Why should it bother him when it was *him* Lexie responded to so passionately? Passion and desire were the only two emotions Lucan was prepared to accept. Love, he had decided long ago, was for fools, male and female, who allowed that emotion to rule their lives.

Including his brother Jordan and Stephanie?

Did Lucan feel *pity* for the two of them because they loved and were in love with each other?

No, of course he didn't. But that was different. Jordan was different from Lucan—didn't seem to remember the complete destruction of their family that had resulted when Alexander had fallen in love with another woman.

If that was what love did to you, the fool it made of you, then Lucan didn't want any part of it.

He stepped back abruptly now. 'Fine.' He nodded grimly. 'I'll make your excuses to the Bartons.'

'Do that,' Lexie rasped, still shaken by the scene that had just occurred. A fraught and emotional scene that had culminated in the chain on her precious necklace being broken.

Almost as if Lucan had known who had given her the locket and had wanted to destroy it and all it represented...

Except there was no way that Lucan could know his father and her grandmother had given her the locket on her sixteenth birthday.

Then why had he been so angry? So *un*-Lucan-like?

What had they been talking about immediately before he'd grabbed at her necklace?

'Can I take it that all discussion of the possibility of the two of us "pursuing a relationship" is now at an end?' she taunted bitterly.

'I don't believe it ever really started.' Lucan looked down at her coldly.

'No.' Lexie's mouth twisted ruefully; Lucan couldn't possibly want to forget that conversation any more strongly than she did!

No doubt some women would have felt flattered by Lucan's suggestion that the two of them stay on here for a few days and pursue an affair—and, no matter what word

Lucan might have chosen to describe it, that was exactly what it would have been. Lexie just felt insulted.

And maybe just a little flattered…?

Maybe just a little.

She might have only known Lucan for two days—was it *really* only two days since she had first met this forcefully arrogant and lethally attractive man?—but she already knew that he was a man who admitted to few, if any, weaknesses. Acknowledging desire for her was definitely a weakness coming from a man whose air of complete detachment proclaimed he didn't need anyone or anything, and never had.

He didn't need her, either, Lexie told herself ruefully; Lucan wanted her, desired her, wanted to go to bed with her, but he didn't *need* her.

Her chin rose as she looked up at him defiantly. 'Isn't it time you were going to the Bartons?'

His mouth tightened at her obvious dismissal. 'They aren't expecting us for another hour.'

'So you thought you might be able to fit in a quickie before you left?' she scorned.

Lucan's eyes narrowed dangerously. 'Someone should have washed your mouth out with soap when you were younger!' he rasped. 'And, just for the record, Lexie—if I ever take you to bed, then it won't be for a quickie!'

The implication of it being the opposite made Lexie's cheeks burn, her breasts tingle and that unfamiliar warmth build between her thighs. 'Luckily for both of us that was always a very big if,' she came back scathingly.

'Luckily, yes.' He nodded abruptly.

They were going nowhere with this conversation, Lexie realised heavily. 'I'm going upstairs to put this away and then to read.' She cradled her broken necklace tightly to her chest. 'I expect you'll have gone if I come back downstairs.'

Lucan deeply regretted that he had ever suggested the two of them do anything about the desire that seemed to flare between them more and more often the longer they were together.

All he had to do now was convince his still raging arousal of how stupid that suggestion had been!

'I expect I will,' he agreed harshly. 'If you change your mind about allowing me to have your necklace repaired—'

'I won't,' she assured him quickly.

The way her fingers tightened instinctively about the piece of jewellery, almost as if she expected Lucan to try to wrench it out of her hand again at any moment, only served to convince him that the locket did have emotional significance to her. To the extent that Lexie didn't even like the thought of Lucan touching it again, let alone allowing him to take it out of her possession…

His jaw tightened. 'My business here is finished, and so, weather permitting, I'm sure you'll be pleased to know we'll be able to leave first thing in the morning.'

'Ecstatically pleased,' she acknowledged tautly.

There was nothing more to be said, Lucan realised. Certainly nothing more he should do.

The fact that he had admitted his desire for Lexie to the extent that he had suggested they stay on here together for a few days and pursue that desire was already much more than he had ever intended to do where this woman was concerned…

Apart from the light that had been left on in the kitchen, the house was in complete darkness when Lucan returned after spending a couple of hours at the Bartons' cottage, assuring him that Lexie had gone to bed in his absence—as she had said she would.

Before or after she had eaten?

Why should it matter to Lucan whether or not Lexie had eaten any supper? She was a grown woman and quite capable of taking care of herself.

He wasn't responsible for Lexie having refused the Bartons' dinner invitation. She had already done that before the conversation that had so angered her and resulted in him accidentally breaking the necklace that obviously meant so much to her.

Nevertheless, Lucan found himself striding past the bedroom he had opted to use for the duration of his stay to Lexie's bedroom, farther down the darkened hallway, where he could see a shaft of light showing beneath the door. She was obviously still awake. But doing what? Reading, as she had suggested she might? Or perhaps sitting there plotting a way she could leave?

Lucan frowned as he heard the sound of movement inside the bedroom. A door closed softly—possibly the one to the adjoining bathroom—and then there was the soft pad of bare feet walking across the carpeted floor.

Was it just Lexie's feet that were bare? Or had she just taken a bath or shower prior to going to bed and was now completely naked on the other side of this door?

Lucan's hands clenched at his sides as he was instantly beset with an image of Lexie's lithely compact body, completely naked, proud up-tilting breasts tipped with those rosy aureoles above a flat and toned stomach, the gentle slope of her hips above a silky triangle of curls nestling between her thighs, slender and graceful legs.

Dear God…!

Lucan shook his head to try and clear it of that erotically seductive image, hoping—needing—to stop the arousal that had instantly gripped his own body. Knowing he had failed as his erection stirred and lengthened, pressing against the restraint of his denims, its hard throb becoming a burning ache.

He should go back to his own bedroom. Now. Away from the temptation of knowing that Lexie was just on the other side of this closed door. Possibly naked…

Lexie looked up with a start as a knock sounded briefly on her bedroom door only a second or so before it was opened, to reveal Lucan silhouetted in the darkness of the hallway outside.

Of course it was Lucan. How could it be anyone else when there were only the two of them in the house?

Besides, who else did Lexie know arrogant enough to walk into someone else's bedroom as if he owned it?

He *did* own it, a little voice inside her head reminded her; Lucan owned the whole of Mulberry Hall!

Oh, shut up, Lexie told that mocking voice. The only thing that mattered was that Lucan had walked into her bedroom without being invited.

She straightened abruptly from where she had been packing the clothes she had worn today into her already full overnight bag, determined that Lucan wouldn't know how vulnerable she felt, wearing only the white vest-top and loose-fitting grey pyjama bottoms that were her usual night attire. Not that she thought Lucan would be in the least disturbed by what she was wearing—no doubt the women who shared his bed usually wore silk and lace, and not much of it at that.

'What do you want, Lucan?' She deliberately held his gaze as she crossed the bedroom to sit on top of the gold brocade cover of the bed—she might be feeling vulnerable talking to him when only wearing her nightclothes, but she wasn't about to dive under the bedcovers as if she were a frightened virgin!

She could see in the softness of the lamplight that Lucan was still wearing the faded denims and grey sweater he'd changed into earlier to go to the Bartons. There was a dark frown between his eyes.

'Lexie, do you think we could just stop the hostilities?'

Every part of Lexie, every alert—alarmed?—nerve, muscle and sinew of her body, told her that she and Lucan were incapable of talking politely to each other. That perhaps they always had been.

'And why would we want to do that?' she prompted warily.

'Because, Lexie, I made a mistake earlier—for which I apologise.' He spoke gruffly.

'And that makes everything OK, does it?'

He breathed out exasperatedly. 'I don't know what else you want from me!'

What *did* Lexie want from Lucan? Something she knew she couldn't have. Ever. Not only because Lucan had already shown himself to be a man who wouldn't allow himself to feel deep emotion for anyone, but also because he was Lucan St Claire. And she was Lexie Hamilton. Granddaughter of the despised Sian Thomas...

She grimaced. 'Which mistake are you apologising for, Lucan?' she asked. 'The suggestion we have an affair? Or the breaking of my necklace when I refused?' Her voice hardened as she remembered the feel of the necklace snapping against her throat, and the shock of seeing it lying broken in Lucan's hand.

His face darkened. 'I didn't— Damn it, you *can't* believe I did that deliberately!'

'No,' she accepted heavily. 'But the fact that it happened

is still…still indicative of how—how *destructive* this attraction between the two of us is.' She shook her head.

'Destructive…?' he repeated slowly.

She nodded. 'We hurt each other, Lucan. Sometimes deliberately, sometimes not, but one way or another we've been doing it since we first met.'

It was because Lucan had wanted to put things right between them that he had knocked on her bedroom door just now. Well…not the only reason, he admitted. But it had certainly entered into the equation. The rift that now existed between himself and Lexie had been at the back of his mind the whole of the time he had been at the Bartons' cottage this evening.

'Please just leave, Lucan,' Lexie advised him wearily now. 'Go back to your own bedroom and leave me alone in mine. That way we can both leave here tomorrow with there being no regrets on either side.'

Lucan's jaw clenched impatiently. He could never remember feeling this frustrated in his life before—so incapable of putting a situation right.

It wasn't helping that Lexie looked so delicately delectable, even edible, as she sat cross-legged on top of the bedclothes, bathed in the golden glow given out by the bedside lamp, the wild darkness of her hair loose about her pale, make-up-less face and the bareness of her slender shoulders. The soft, enticing swell of her breasts, with their deep rose tips, was clearly visible beneath the soft material of her white vest top.

His gaze rose to meet and hold hers as he took a step farther into the bedroom. Followed by another when she didn't object. Then another. Until Lucan stood beside the bed looking down at her.

'Do you really want me to leave, Lexie?' he prompted huskily.

Did she? Did she want Lucan to turn around and leave her alone here? Alone and aching?

No, of course Lexie didn't want Lucan to leave. She just knew that he should. For both their sakes.

The house had seemed strangely empty after Lucan had left earlier this evening. Giving Lexie time to think—time to realise how attracted she was to him. How she wanted more from Lucan than he was willing to give. Than he was capable of giving. Not just to her, she had realised, but to any woman.

Whatever the reason—possibly a love affair that had gone wrong in his youth, or maybe simply his parents' broken marriage—she was sure that at some time in the past Lucan had made a conscious decision to shut himself off from emotion.

Except Lexie had seen him laugh several times during the last two days. Usually *at* something she had said or done rather than with her, admittedly, but nevertheless those moments of humour had enabled Lexie to see another side of Lucan. A boyish, softer side it was all too easy to find attractive, even irresistible.

And Lexie didn't want to be attracted to Lucan. Didn't want to find him irresistible. What she wanted was to continue thinking of him as the cold and ruthless man she had believed him to be before she'd met him.

And she could no longer do that…

Every time she tried to slot Lucan back into that unlikeable role another memory would come along to destroy it. Lucan teasing her. Lucan laughing huskily. Lucan with pain in those dark eyes earlier today, rather than the contempt she would have expected, as he'd stood in the west gallery looking up at the portrait of his father.

Most of all Lexie couldn't erase the memory of Lucan almost making love to her…

Lucan might be a lot of the things she had previously thought him to be—arrogant, bossy and remote being only three of them!—but she only had to think of the passion that had flared so unexpectedly between the two of them the previous evening, and again several times today, to know that he wasn't *only* cold and ruthless.

To know also that her own heated, out-of-control response to Lucan was totally off the scale of any of her previous lukewarm relationships.

'You're taking a long time to answer, Lexie,' he said huskily now.

Because Lexie knew that what she *should* do was repeat her request for Lucan to go. That he should leave her bedroom now, before she made the biggest mistake of her life.

She couldn't do it!

Just as she could no longer bear even the thought of going back to London tomorrow and never seeing Lucan again…

Her throat moved convulsively as she swallowed. 'Did you have a pleasant evening with John and Cathy?'

Lucan frowned at this abrupt change of subject. 'Very pleasant.' He nodded. 'They were sorry you were unable to be there because you had gone to bed with a headache,' he added dryly.

Lexie gave a rueful smile. 'Was that the excuse you gave them for my absence?'

Lucan grimaced. 'Well, I could hardly tell them the truth, could I? That you had gone to bed because I had been so damned obnoxious you couldn't bear the thought of spending the evening in my company.'

'That isn't true!' Lexie protested breathlessly.

'Isn't it?' Lucan moved to sit on the side of the bed, before reaching out to curve his hand against the softness of Lexie's cheek as he gazed deeply into her wide blue eyes. 'Something about you makes me do things, say things—cruel things—that I wouldn't normally do or say.' He gave a self-disgusted shake of his head.

'The fact that I'm infuriating, impossible and stubborn, perhaps?' she suggested huskily.

Lucan wished those were the *only* things he thought of this woman! Unfortunately, Lexie's actions also showed her to be loyal—he knew it was loyalty to Premier Personnel that had made her agree to come to Mulberry Hall with him in the first place, courageous in the face of Lucan's displeasure, which had been known to make grown men quake in their shoes. Lexie was also intelligent, witty, feisty and so beautiful that just looking at her now intensified his arousal to almost painful levels.

'No.' He gave a rueful shake of his head and raised both his hands to place them gently against her temples and smooth back the silky dark hair from her face. 'It's because I want to make love to you so much I can't think straight,' he admitted huskily.

She moistened her lips with the tip of her delicate pink tongue. 'You do…?'

Lucan nodded, unable to break his gaze away from those parted lips. 'Lexie, I want—need—to make love to you so badly at this moment that I can't think of anything else!'

Lexie's heart leapt, thundering in her chest at the admission, and her skin was suddenly warm and ultra-sensitive as she felt the touch, the heat, of Lucan's hands as they threaded lightly in her hair. As she saw the raw hunger burning in his eyes, in the tense, raw angles of his face.

A hunger that was echoed deep inside Lexie.

Even more deeply than the knowledge that making love with Lucan, to Lucan, having him make love with and to her, was exactly what she shouldn't allow to happen…

CHAPTER TEN

'SAY SOMETHING, Lexie…!' he groaned achingly.

'Shh,' she soothed huskily, as one of her hands moved up to cup the side of his face.

A hot, quivering awareness coursed the length of her arm and down her spine as she stared up into the heat of Lucan's eyes.

Her breasts were tingling in anticipation as she imagined Lucan's hands, his mouth, on her there, the nipples hardening to a burning, sensual ache, and there was a low throbbing between her thighs as she felt herself swell there as those delicate tissues became damp, wet in invitation.

She wanted Lucan to make love to her. Wanted to make love to him. Just once wanted to touch, to caress, to taste every single beautiful inch of him…!

Her gaze continued to hold his as she moved up onto her knees and slowly raised her hands to touch his chest, so close now she was able to feel his hard warmth and the rapid beat of his heart through the thin wool of his sweater.

It wasn't close enough. Lexie wanted to touch the bareness of Lucan's skin. To feel the quivering response of his flesh against her fingertips and palms, her lips and tongue.

Her gaze continued to hold his as her hands moved down

to the bottom of his sweater to slowly, oh-so-slowly, pull the woollen garment up and above the flatness of his defined stomach to his muscled chest.

'Lexie?' Lucan questioned again gruffly.

'Please don't talk, Lucan.' She placed gentle fingertips against his firm lips. 'It always ends up in an argument and one of us always says the wrong thing.' She turned her attention to the light dusting of dark chest hair ending in a V at the base of his stomach before disappearing beneath the waistband of his denims.

His skin was so hard and muscled beneath the touch of her fingers—testament to the fact that Lucan didn't spend all of his time in a boardroom! Lexie was drawn, tempted to touch the tight buds hidden amongst that dusting of silky dark hair.

She glanced up at Lucan when he drew in a raggedly sharp breath as her fingertips grazed across them. 'You like that...?'

'Oh, yes...!' he encouraged achingly, cheeks flushed, a nerve pulsing in the rigidness of his jaw, hunger burning in the depths of those dark, dark eyes as he continued to look at her from beneath lowered lids.

Her head slowly lowered so she could taste Lucan there, and his hand moved up instinctively to cup her head, his back arching, lids closing, as her lips skimmed across his chest. The air was cool, arousing, as it brushed against the residue of moisture left on the surface of his skin from those caressing lips and tongue.

Lucan released her only long enough to pull his sweater up and over his head, before tossing it down onto the carpeted floor, his body on fire as Lexie's arms now moved about his waist, her hands a fiery caress against his shoulders and down the length of his back as she continued to kiss and caress his chest with her lips and tongue.

Lucan wanted—needed—to touch her, too…

Lexie gasped hoarsely as one of Lucan's hands cupped beneath her breast, over her vest top, and the soft pad of his thumb lightly caressed that aching tip, sending rivulets of pleasure down her body to pool, burn, between her aching and needy thighs.

Lucan was breathing raggedly as he pulled back slightly. 'Lexie, let me look at you,' he said hotly.

Lexie's hands shook slightly as she sat back on her heels to pull the vest top over her head and discard it, her cheeks becoming hot as Lucan looked down at her semi-nakedness with dark and hungry eyes.

Her breasts seemed to swell under the intensity of that gaze, the already puckered nipples hardening to ripe berries against her otherwise pale skin. Asking, begging to be in the heat of Lucan's mouth!

'You're so beautiful, Lexie.' Lucan's breath was a warm caress against those aroused nipples, and his hands cupped beneath both her breasts to hold them up in sacrifice to his tongue as he paid homage to first one sensitive peak and then the other.

Lexie could only cling mindlessly to his muscled shoulders as sensation surged through her and down her, to clench in hot, sweet pleasure between her thighs. As Lucan sucked one of her nipples strongly, deeply into the heat of his mouth, that pleasure became a burning ache as she felt the need to have Lucan inside her.

'Lucan…!' Lexie groaned that need as her fingers became entangled in the dark thickness of his hair, holding him to her as her back arched, lifting her breasts and tilting her nipple deeper into the heat of his hungry mouth.

Lucan drew on her hungrily and allowed his hands to move to her waist. Lexie's skin was like silken velvet beneath his touch as he pushed the waistband of those loose-fitting pyjama bottoms lower down her thighs, exposing her pelvic bone and then a silky triangle of curls before he sought the tiny centre of pleasure between her legs.

Lucan stroked it, again and again, and Lexie's breath caught in her throat in small needy groans as each stroke brought her closer to release, but never quite close enough.

Her body tensed as she trembled in anticipation. 'Lucan, please!' Lexie's hands tightened in his hair as she shifted slightly, legs parting wider, her hips arching into him in a more urgent plea.

His mouth left her breast, trailing heated kisses upwards along that silken slope, and he was able to feel her trembling response as his tongue rasped against the sensitive cord in her throat and then up to her mouth. His other hand tangled in the heavy thickness of her hair, holding her as his mouth claimed hers, his tongue surging hotly into her mouth, capturing Lexie's keening cry of pleasure as she found her release.

She had barely recovered when his fingers surged inside her. Her muscles clenched, holding him there as they thrust into her slowly, rhythmically, giving and at the same time taking all she had to give. His mouth left hers and returned to claim the ripe berry of her nipple in that same dancing rhythm, once again sending her over that plateau of sensual pleasure.

'Oh, God—oh, God—oh, God…!' Lexie's head dropped forward onto Lucan's chest minutes later, her fingers clinging, digging into his muscled shoulders, as the pleasurable ripples of release continued to shake her body.

Lucan's lips were a sensual caress along the line of her jaw as he gently eased his fingers from inside her, teeth gently biting the softness of her lobe before his tongue stroked the shell-like shape of her ear and his fingers once more circled that throb between her thighs.

Lexie trembled, her back tensing, as she felt a quiver of response deep inside her. 'I can't,' she groaned weakly. 'Lucan, I really can't...'

'You can,' he encouraged softly, and moved back slightly so that he could help her to lie down on top of the bed-clothes, remaining up on his knees as he lightly gripped the waistband of her pyjama bottoms and began to slide them down her thighs, over her knees, before pulling them fully from her body and dropping them beside the bed.

Naked now, bathed in the golden glow of the bedside lamp, Lexie felt as well as saw the way Lucan's dark and devouring gaze moved slowly, hungrily, over every inch of her naked body—her breasts, the flatness of her stomach, curvaceous hips and thighs.

He looked every inch a pagan god as he knelt above her, his hair falling wildly across his brow, eyes dark and stormy, his face all harsh and yet sensual angles, his chest and shoulders hard and with rippling muscle.

'Take off your denims, Lucan,' she encouraged huskily.

His eyes glowed warmly in challenge. 'You take them off for me,' he invited gruffly.

Lexie swallowed hard as she slowly moved up onto her haunches, unable to look away from that dark and com-pelling gaze. She reached out for the button fastening at his waist, feeling the quivering response of his stomach muscles as she inadvertently touched bare flesh before managing to slowly slide down the zipper, realising as she did so that there was no way she was going to get the body-hugging denims down over his hips and muscled thighs without help from Lucan.

But maybe she didn't need to take them off completely just yet...

She caught her bottom lip between her teeth as her gaze lowered to the black boxers revealed by parting the two sides of the zip, the soft cotton clinging lovingly to the hard bulge beneath. Its hardness pulsed and surged upwards as Lexie cupped Lucan there, before her fingers stroked that hard length with slow circular caresses that made Lucan harder still, allowing Lexie to feel that pumping surge of his blood against her fingertips.

'Touch me, Lexie!' Lucan's voice was a harsh growl. 'I need to feel your hands on my skin!'

'Lie back,' she encouraged softly, moving to kneel beside him once he had lain back against the pillows. He allowed Lexie to peel the two garments slowly down his body before she moved back between Lucan's thighs and looked down at him admiringly from beneath lowered lashes.

Beautiful.

There was no other word to describe the hard and muscled contours of Lucan's completely naked body.

Beautiful like a Greek statue come to life—every part of him in proportion: his shoulders and chest wide, waist tapered, his arousal long and hard as it jutted out from a nest of dark curls, his legs long and perfect.

Lexie's hungry gaze returned to his thrusting arousal, her tongue moving moistly across her lips as that long and silken hardness instantly responded to her interest. She was able to see the blood surging beneath the surface as it pulsed, lifting up towards her in invitation.

An invitation she couldn't resist...

He'd died and gone to heaven.

Where else could Lucan be when his imaginings on that

first day he had met Lexie, of having the mind-shattering heat and pleasure of Lexie's mouth against his pulsing shaft, the lap of her tongue along his throbbing length, had come true?

Maybe he wasn't in heaven, after all. Maybe he had just lost his mind…

If this was insanity then Lucan knew he would be happy to remain out of his mind for the rest of his life!

Lexie's hands grasped him firmly as the rasp of her tongue moved slowly—excruciatingly slowly—along the length of his shaft from base to tip. Lucan groaned as it dipped and tasted the delicacy of the tip.

'You like that, too…?'

Lucan could barely focus on Lexie, he liked it so much! 'Does *more* answer your question?' he groaned huskily.

'Oh, yes.' Lexie chuckled softly, her fingers curled lightly about that pulsing shaft as she sat back and caressed him, her eyes a deep navy blue as she watched his responses from beneath dark, silky lashes, her cheeks flushed and her lips—God, those plump and pouting lips!—once again driving him insane.

Lucan's fingers clenched into the bedcovers beneath him as he watched the expression on Lexie's face even as she watched him, watched his responses to her caresses. She was obviously enjoying pleasuring him as much as Lucan was enjoying being pleasured.

'I want to be inside you when I come, Lexie,' he told her gruffly when she gave him a slightly reproachful look as he sat up to lift her gently but firmly away from him, before moving to take her into his arms.

Lucan wanted to be inside her…

The sexual haze faded from Lexie's head. Not because she didn't want all of Lucan's silken hardness inside her—

Lexie ached for that. No, her sudden wariness was for another reason entirely.

She was an avid reader, enjoyed nothing more than a good love story, and in every book she had ever read where the hero realised the heroine's lack of experience only as he pierced her virginity the man reacted in one of two ways: accusing, because he suspected entrapment, or emotional at being the heroine's first lover because he was deeply in love with her.

Lexie knew that Lucan wasn't in love with her—which left only accusations…

'Lexie?'

She moistened dry lips, a pained frown creasing her brow as she met his concerned gaze. 'I think I ought to ask how you feel about being a woman's first lover.'

Lucan stared at her blankly for several tense seconds. '*Your* first lover?' he finally realised.

She grimaced. 'Yes.'

How did Lucan feel about being Lexie's first lover? How would *any* man feel at the thought of being this beautiful woman's first lover?

Probably exactly the way Lucan did—privileged. And a little surprised.

'I had no idea,' he murmured softly. 'You're so outspoken, so self-confident, it never occurred to me there hadn't been another man in your bed.'

'Yes… Well…' A delicate blush heightened her cheeks. 'Technically speaking, this isn't my bed, either.'

'For the moment it is.'

She nodded. 'I just thought I ought to mention the thing to you before—well, before we go any further. Every woman has to start somewhere, right?' She brightened. 'So it might just as well be with a man who knows what he's doing.'

'Just as well,' Lucan echoed gruffly, not sure that he wasn't going to smile at this typically Lexie comment, at the realisation that no other man had ever made love to this lovely woman in the way that he had. In the way that he was going to.

And Lexie had never touched another man in the intimate way she had him just now. Just the thought of that possibility was enough to increase the aching throb between his thighs.

'And I can really do without you getting either angry or sentimental over it,' she warned him firmly.

'Angry or sentimental…?' Lucan repeated dryly.

'Well—okay. It's unlikely, you being you, that you're going to feel the second of those emotions.' She gave a rueful shrug. 'But I don't want to take any chances.'

Lucan looked down at her quizzically. 'Me being me?'

'You know, Lucan, this conversation would go along much quicker if you just stopped repeating everything I say!' She glared at him reprovingly.

It was no good. Lucan couldn't hold back his smile, his laughter, any longer.

He should be annoyed at that crack—'you being you'—but the truth of the matter was he was too damned bemused by this woman to feel annoyed about anything she said.

In the past, lovemaking had always seemed rather a serious business to Lucan. Something to be mutually enjoyed, certainly, but ultimately lacking in any emotion except the need to satisfy the lust he and his partner felt for each other. Only Lexie, a woman like no other woman Lucan had ever met, could bring him to task, make him want to laugh, in the middle of lovemaking.

'I'm not sure I want to be laughed at, either!' She gave him a reproving frown.

'I'm not laughing *at* you, Lexie,' Lucan assured as he took her gently in his arms and held her. 'I'm laughing *with* you!'

That would certainly be a change, Lexie acknowledged ruefully. A very pleasant one now that Lucan knew she was a virgin.

'You're an extraordinary woman, Lexie Hamilton,' he murmured into the thickness of her hair.

'Something else we agree on!' she came back sassily as her self-confidence returned.

'No, you were right the first time: we *do* end up arguing every time we talk!' Lucan gave her a wry smile. 'And to answer your question,' he continued huskily, 'I would very much enjoy being your first lover.'

Her eyes widened. 'You would…?'

He nodded. 'Very much.'

It suddenly struck Lexie as being very funny that she was sitting there stark naked, with a man equally naked— with *Lucan* gorgeously, wonderfully naked—engaging in a conversation as to whether or not they should continue making love together. How ridiculous was that?

'Lexie…?' Lucan prompted indulgently as she let out a sudden burst of laughter.

'Sorry. I just— It's—' She broke off as she was consumed with another bout of laughter.

Out of sheer relief, probably, Lexie recognised ruefully, at Lucan's unexpected but very welcome reaction to her revelation of still being a virgin. Whatever the reason, she couldn't seem to stop laughing—and seconds later she felt the reverberation of Lucan's chest against her as he also began to chuckle.

CHAPTER ELEVEN

'How do you feel about going downstairs for a late-night snack?' Lucan lay back on the bed, Lexie's head on his shoulder, her arm across his abdomen. He held her curved tightly against his side, their laughter having finally subsided.

Cathy Barton had prepared a delicious meal earlier this evening, but Lucan really hadn't been hungry enough to do Cathy's cooking justice following his argument with Lexie. He had a feeling that Lexie hadn't eaten anything this evening, either.

Besides, he would like to savour the thought of being Lexie's first lover a little longer…

'What?' A slightly bemused Lexie raised her head to look up at him.

'Did you eat anything after I left earlier this evening?' Lucan prompted softly.

'Well…no. But wouldn't you like to—? I mean, I know *I* did—several times—but you certainly didn't, and—'

Lucan shifted slightly so that Lexie was the one who now lay back on the pillows, with him looking down at her. 'Lexie, if you're trying, in your own inimitable style, to say that you had multiple orgasms earlier, and I haven't had any yet, then—'

'Lucan!' She buried her flushed face against his chest in obvious embarrassment.

Endearingly so, Lucan recognised indulgently. 'Well, are you?' he prompted teasingly, and was rewarded by a muttered 'yes' against his chest. The warmth of Lexie's breath was a warm and sensual caress on his bare flesh. 'There's no rush, Lexie. After all, we have all night,' he assured her huskily.

She looked up at him with wide blue eyes. 'All night…?'

'*Now* who's repeating everything I say?' he teased.

'Well, yes—but… *All night,* Lucan?' Her tone was a mixture of awe and anticipation.

'I don't see why not—as long as you feed me the occasional morsel of food to keep my strength up,' he drawled softly.

'Let's go and eat!' She moved out of his arms to sit up.

The sight of Lexie's pouting and naked breasts instantly caused Lucan to review his decision concerning a need for food right now. They could easily delay eating for another fifteen minutes—possibly half an hour…an hour…

An option he had realised too late, as Lexie stood up to modestly turn her back towards him and pull a robe on over her nakedness. Her uncharacteristic shyness instantly reminded Lucan that for all her outspoken self-confidence, Lexie really wasn't one of the sophisticated women who usually shared his bed.

And they really did have all night…

Lexie was amazed ten minutes later at how relaxed she felt, sitting in the warmth of the kitchen with Lucan, snacking on the cheese and biscuits Cathy Barton had included in the box of food yesterday, and drinking strong coffee.

It made Lucan seem less like the powerhouse of energy she had first met, and more like the man who was about to become her first lover...

Possibly helped by the darkness of his hair still falling rakishly across his brow rather than being brushed back in the severe style he usually favoured. Or it might have been the casual denims and jumper he had pulled back on before coming downstairs. Or the comfortable way they had set about preparing the food and coffee together a few minutes ago. Or the warmth of the smile that curved the corners of Lucan's sculpted mouth every time he glanced across the table at her.

Whatever the reason, Lexie felt at ease in his company. 'This is nice.'

'Yes.' He nodded. 'Yes, it is.'

'There's no need to seem so surprised!' Lexie laughed softly.

Lucan *was* surprised at how pleasant it was just to sit there and eat a snack with Lexie. At how pleasant it was to just sit there and do anything with Lexie.

He felt completely relaxed—a rare commodity in a life that was usually hectic in the extreme, with no time for just sitting back and 'smelling the roses', as his mother had put it the last time she'd lectured him concerning his need to relax more and work less.

Considering the tension between them from the beginning of their acquaintance, Lexie Hamilton was the last person Lucan would ever have thought he could relax with. And in the kitchen at Mulberry Hall, of all places!

'It's very good, Lexie,' he assured her huskily.

She returned his gaze quizzically. 'But you *are* surprised?'

'You're always surprising me, Lexie,' he stated truthfully.

Which was probably part of her attraction, Lucan recognised consideringly; he never knew what Lexie was going to say or do next!

'In what way?' she prompted curiously.

'In every way!'

'So.' She looked over at him from beneath dark lashes. 'Will I be your first virgin?'

Lucan's laugh was completely spontaneous as he stared across the table at her incredulously. 'Will you be—?' He gave a slightly dazed shake of his head. 'I really haven't met anyone quite like you before, Lexie.'

'But that's good, isn't it?'

Lucan wasn't sure that 'good' was exactly the way he would have described this experience. It was certainly novel to talk in this frank and open way with a woman he had every intention of making love to—several times—before the night was over. Tomorrow, too, if he could persuade Lexie into reconsidering their decision to leave in the morning.

'It's certainly different,' he finally conceded dryly.

'Good or bad different?'

'Good. I think,' he added with a frown.

Her eyes glowed with laughter. 'But you aren't sure?'

'I don't think I've been really sure of anything since the moment I first met you,' he acknowledged ruefully. 'You obviously weren't present when they were handing out the reserve gene!'

'Oh, I was probably just hiding behind a door,' she dismissed unconcernedly.

'Right.' Lucan straightened in his chair. 'Then, yes, Lexie, you will be my first virgin.'

She tilted her head. 'And how do you feel about that?'

'Nervous.'

'What?' She sat back to eye him disbelievingly, absolutely astounded that Lucan had admitted to feeling nervous about anything.

The very first thing Lexie had noticed about him had been the air of power that he wore like an invisible cloak. An inborn self-confidence that said he knew who and what he was, and dared anyone to challenge that knowledge.

He gave a derisive smile. 'Try looking at it from my point of view, Lexie. You're—what...? Twenty-something?'

'Four.'

'Hmm. And no doubt in those twenty-four years you've read books and seen films that depict lovemaking as being a wild and wonderful experience?'

A delicate blush warmed her cheeks. 'No doubt.'

Lucan nodded. 'What if the reality doesn't measure up to the things they write in books and show in the movies?'

'It has so far!'

He smiled. 'You're doing wonders for my ego, Lexie.'

She eyed him teasingly. 'Your ego doesn't need any more stroking!'

He gave a lazy smile. 'You sound very sure of that.'

Well, of course Lexie was sure of that. She only had to look at him as he sat across the table from her, so relaxed and sure of himself, just like a big, sleepy cat. The untamed variety, of course. Lucan St Claire was a law unto himself and always would be—a man who indulged in sensual relationships without ever becoming emotionally involved.

Which suited Lexie perfectly. She only had this one night with Lucan, and would never see him again—could never see him again—once the two of them returned to London tomorrow.

'Have any of your other women ever had cause to complain?' she teased.

He frowned. 'Lexie—'

'Don't tell me—it simply isn't done to talk about the other women you've been to bed with?'

He looked slightly bemused. 'Believe me, nothing that's happened with you has ever happened to me before.'

'Really…?' She caught her bottom lip between her teeth and stood up to move slowly round the table to where Lucan sat, pushing her robe back over her hips and placing her hands on his shoulders for support as she settled herself across his muscled thighs.

'That isn't my ego you're stroking, Lexie,' Lucan drawled huskily as she moved slowly, oh-so-slowly, against the rigid hardness of the arousal pressing against his denims.

'No?' She gave him a warm and sensuous smile as she continued that rocking movement.

His eyes darkened almost to black as he parted the top folds of her robe to bare the pertness of her breasts. 'You really are very beautiful here, Lexie,' he murmured softly, and he lowered his head to lightly kiss each aroused nipple in turn, before concentrating his attentions on just one.

Lexie's breath caught in her throat. 'I need you to make love to me, Lucan,' she groaned achingly, her fingers becoming entangled in the darkness of his hair as she held him to her.

'Here?'

'Anywhere!'

Lucan truly had never met a woman like Lexie. So open. So totally honest. About herself and her needs.

The same needs were raging within him—and had been, he now acknowledged, since the moment he'd first met her.

Needs they both became totally lost in as they kissed and touched. Heatedly. Wildly. Lips and hands seeking and finding every pleasure point. Every touch, every caress, driving their passion higher and then higher still as desire spiralled out of control. As their need raged totally out of control.

Lucan's hands cupped beneath Lexie's bottom as he surged to his feet, her hands clinging to his shoulders, her legs wrapped tightly about his waist as he strode from the kitchen and carried her back up the stairs to her bedroom, to lay her gently down on the bed.

Lexie cast aside her robe and watched as Lucan threw off his own clothes before joining her on the bed, nudging her legs gently apart before kneeling between her thighs to part her dark curls and bare her to his dark and searing gaze.

'God, you're beautiful, Lexie…' he groaned, his hands moving lightly across her burning flesh as his head began to lower. 'So damned beautiful,' he said achingly, his breath a warm caress against her sensitivity.

Lexie gasped at the first touch of Lucan's mouth against her heat. He laved her with his tongue, and the sensation, the pleasure, was unlike anything she had ever experienced before. Deeper, even stronger than during their earlier lovemaking.

Her head fell back against the pillows as she felt the onset of orgasm surging through her, burning her, as pleasure ripped through her, seeming never-ending as Lucan drank, lapped up every last vestige of that release before moving up to position himself between her thighs.

'Take me inside you, Lexie,' he encouraged gruffly. 'Take me before I lose my mind!'

Lexie needed no further encouragement, and she curled her fingers about him and began to guide him inside her, inch by beautiful inch. Her delicate folds widened, stretching to accommodate the width and length of him, until he reached the barrier of her virginity.

Lucan was breathing hard, determined to maintain control, to ensure that Lexie enjoyed her first experience of lovemaking.

That control didn't come easy. Lucan was raging inside as his shaft surged, pulsed with the need to take what was already his!

He leant his weight on his elbows as he looked down at her. 'I don't want to hurt you!' he groaned.

'You won't.' There was complete trust in her eyes as she gazed up at him.

He rested the dampness of his forehead against hers, breathing deeply through his nose. 'I might—'

'You won't,' she repeated with certainty.

Lucan's chest swelled at her complete faith in his ability not to hurt her. 'Hold on to my shoulders,' he encouraged huskily, and he drew his thighs back slightly before thrusting those last few inches, breaching the barrier of her virginity as she took him fully inside her.

Lucan heard Lexie gasp, felt her body tensing as her fingernails dug briefly into his flesh before she relaxed again, allowing the softness of her inner folds to wrap around him. Hot, so very hot, and velvet-soft. He grasped her hips, his mouth capturing hers as he began to thrust slowly, rhythmically inside her.

Pleasure engulfed him as his thrusts deepened, hardened, drowning Lucan in pleasure, in ecstasy unlike anything he had ever known before. He felt his release building, higher and higher, and Lexie's keening cries told him that she was fast approaching her own climax.

Her legs wrapped about his waist as she tensed beneath him, tightening around him as her orgasm ripped through her, those clenching spasms taking Lucan with her. And he felt the heat of his own release surge down the length of his shaft and burst inside her in hot and never-ending pleasure.

'Wow…' Lexie breathed weakly long minutes later, when she finally found enough breath to be able to talk at all. Her hands moved in a long, slow caress across and down the broad width of Lucan's back as he lay still, above and inside her.

Lucan chuckled huskily. 'That was—'

'Please don't burst my happy bubble by telling me I was rubbish at it!' she groaned.

'—incredible!' he finished softly as he moved up on his elbows to look down at her. '*You're* incredible, Lexie,' he assured her gruffly, his expression serious as his hands moved to cradle either side of her face. 'Did I hurt you?'

'No.' Lexie had felt only a small pinch of pain, brief and quickly forgotten as she became caught up in the pleasure of having Lucan deeply inside her.

Lucan didn't look reassured. 'You're probably a little sore?'

Lexie still felt full, completely filled by Lucan, and it certainly wasn't a painful feeling. The opposite, in fact, as her sensitive inner muscles continued to spasm and clench pleasurably about him.

'Not at all.' She reached up to gently smooth the dark hair from Lucan's brow. 'In fact, as soon as you're able, I would like to do it all over again!'

'Greedy little baggage,' he murmured admiringly.

'Mmm.' Her legs tightened about his waist. 'I intend keeping you exactly where you are for the rest of the night!' She wasn't about to waste a single minute, a second, of the one night she would have with Lucan.

He gave a rueful shake of his head. 'Your honesty is overwhelming.'

Lexie stilled. Her honesty…?

She had been completely honest about her enjoyment of their lovemaking, but about everything else…?

Lexie hadn't been honest with Lucan about any other part of her life!

She didn't work as a temp for Premier Personnel—she helped to run it with her parents. It wasn't true that there was no other temp available to send to the St Claire Corporation—Lexie had deliberately decided to go and work there herself for three days, in order to settle her long-held curiosity concerning the St Claire family itself. Most especially about the head of that family, Lucan St Claire.

Well, she had done a lot more than settle her curiosity about Lucan. A lot, lot more.

'Lexie…?' There was a dark frown between Lucan's eyes as Lexie slid her legs down the backs of his thighs to rest her feet on the bed. Her hand fell limply back to her side. 'Are you having regrets, after all?'

Not the sort Lucan obviously meant—but, yes, Lexie *was* having regrets.

Lots of them. Mainly she was regretting that she had ever begun this dangerous subterfuge. Because if Lucan ever found out exactly who she was, her connection to Sian Thomas, then he really was going to hate her.

Lexie didn't want Lucan to hate her. And she didn't still hate him…

How could she ever have thought she could make love with Lucan—physically take what he had to give—the pleasure she had already glimpsed so fleetingly on those other occasions when he had held her in his arms and kissed her—and then just walk away without there being any repercussions to herself?

How could she have been so naive?

How could she have been so stupid not to have realised she was already in love with him…?

CHAPTER TWELVE

'LEXIE, what's wrong?' Lucan frowned when she could only stare up at him in shock. 'Talk to me, damn it!' He grasped her shoulders and shook her as she didn't respond.

Talk to him? Lexie wasn't sure she would ever be able to talk to Lucan again, let alone coherently. She was in love with him! Had fallen in love with Lucan St Claire—the man she had always hated. The one man who believed he had every reason to despise all her family.

Lexie had heard it said that there was a very thin line between love and hate...

How could this have happened? *Why* had it happened? What mad and vengeful god—goddess—could have wished this upon her?

'Lucan—could you move?' Lexie pleaded desperately as the food she had eaten earlier rose like bile in the back of her throat. The feeling grew worse as she was totally overwhelmed by Lucan's close proximity. By the fact that his body was still intimately joined with hers. 'Now, Lucan!' she begged. 'I—I think I'm going to be sick!'

Lucan barely had time to disengage and roll to the side before Lexie stood up to dash madly—nakedly—to the adjoining bathroom. The door slammed shut behind her, followed seconds later by the sound of forceful retching.

Lucan fell heavily back against the pillows to stare

sightlessly up at the ceiling, feeling slightly nauseous himself at the possibility that it had been their lovemaking that had made Lexie ill.

Had he hurt her, after all?

Was she in so much pain it had actually made her physically sick?

Or was it something else? Possibly the realisation of what had just happened between the two of them had affected her so dramatically?

Lucan sat up, only to come to an abrupt halt and feel a painful wrenching in his gut as he saw the smear of blood on the sheet beside him in evidence of Lexie's innocence.

Lucan's expression was grim as he stood up to pull his denims on over his nakedness, before padding across the room barefoot to knock softly on the bathroom door. He turned the handle. 'Lexie…'

'Don't come in here!' Lexie cried desperately as she realised Lucan's intention. Wasn't it enough that Lucan must know she was in here throwing up the food and drink she'd had earlier, without the added humiliation of having Lucan see her actually bent naked over the toilet? 'Go away, Lucan,' she instructed him crossly. She glared across to where she could see Lucan—as he must surely be able to see her!—where he stood on the other side of the partially opened bathroom door.

'Do you need any help—?'

'To be sick?' she scorned. 'I don't think so, thank you very much! Just go away and leave me alone,' she repeated impatiently.

'I can't do that—'

'Of course you can.' Lexie turned to grab a towel from the rack and wrap it about herself before standing up. 'It's easy, Lucan. You just close the damned door and turn around and walk away!'

'No.'

'What do you mean, no?' Lexie flushed the toilet before marching across the bathroom to wrench the door open and glare up at Lucan. At Lucan so sexily attractive dressed only in faded denims that Lexie's knees went weak just looking at him!

His chest was so broad and muscled, his stomach so flat and toned, and those denims rested on narrow hips above long and muscled legs. Shifting her gaze quickly back to Lucan's face wasn't really any help either, when his hair was still slightly mussed and falling sexily across his forehead. His eyes were dark and full of concern, and that firm mouth was just asking to be kissed.

Well…asking to be kissed if Lexie's own mouth hadn't felt so unpleasant after she'd been so thoroughly sick!

She turned back into the bathroom and crossed over to the sink to brush her teeth.

'I mean no, Lexie,' Lucan repeated firmly behind her. 'We need to talk.'

'We don't need to do anything of the sort!' She rinsed her mouth with water before turning to look at him. 'I've obviously eaten something that disagreed with me—'

'Cheese and biscuits?' Lucan drawled sceptically.

Lexie glared up at him. 'Something!' She pushed past him to cross the bedroom and pick up her robe from where it had been thrown onto the carpet earlier.

Lucan leant against the bathroom doorway and watched her through narrowed lids. The dark wildness of Lexie's hair just added to the deathly pallor of her cheeks, but neither of those things detracted in the least from how sexy she looked, wearing only a very inadequate bath towel, with the swell of her breasts visible above and her legs bare and shapely beneath.

His thighs stirred in renewed arousal as she turned away to slip her arms into the robe, before pulling the towel off and tying the belt firmly at her slender waist. Her breasts were outlined against the silk material as she turned to face him.

Lucan pushed away from the doorframe, eyes narrowed grimly at the inappropriateness of his arousal. 'What just happened, Lexie?'

Her chin rose. 'I told you—'

'You don't get food poisoning from eating fresh cheese and biscuits,' he dismissed firmly.

Lexie wished that Lucan would put some more clothes on; it was very disconcerting trying to have a conversation with a man who looked as sexy as Lucan did right now. With a man whose arousal was unmistakably outlined against those close-fitting denims.

With a man Lexie had realised only minutes ago she was in love with...

She thrust trembling hands into the pockets of her robe. 'I do,' she answered firmly. 'Obviously.'

He gave a slow shake of his head. 'It wasn't the cheese and biscuits that made you sick.'

'Then what did, Dr St Claire?' She eyed him scathingly.

His mouth thinned at the taunt. 'I was hoping you could tell me that.'

'Oh, no.' Lexie shook her head scornfully. 'You're the one who seems to think he has all the answers!'

Lucan breathed deeply through his nose, having no intention of allowing Lexie to goad him into losing his temper. As she seemed so set on doing... 'Maybe you regret what just happened?'

She frowned. 'I already said I didn't.'

'Before you were violently ill!' Lucan bit out harshly, positive that Lexie was lying to him—that the honesty he had remarked upon earlier was completely lacking at this moment. He just had no idea why that was.

'Obviously eating cheese at midnight doesn't agree with me.'

'I have already discounted that as the cause, Lexie.'

'But I haven't!' Those blue eyes flashed angrily. 'Would you just *go*, Lucan?' She grimaced. 'I'm feeling pretty awful and I'd like to go to bed.'

'Alone?'

'Well, of course alone! Unless you're feeling a perverted desire to make love to a sick woman?'

Lucan's desire for Lexie's wasn't in the least perverted— just continuous, it seemed. A never-ending ache that hadn't been in the least assuaged by their lovemaking earlier. It would perhaps never be completely satisfied, no matter how deeply or how often he made love with and to this particular woman...

His jaw tightened. 'Perhaps I should sleep in here, in case you're ill again in the night.'

'Haven't I just made it obvious how much I hate having an audience when I'm ill?' she snapped.

Lucan gave an abrupt inclination of his head. 'You made it just as obvious earlier that you couldn't wait for us to make love again.'

Lexie drew in a sharp breath. She had said that, hadn't she? Before she had realised her feelings for this man. Before she had realised she was in love with Lucan St Claire, fifteenth Duke of Stourbridge, a man she had always considered her bitterest enemy. As she and the whole of her family were his...

'Post-coital euphoria,' she dismissed tersely, before turning away. Just looking at Lucan was enough to make her long for pre-coital, coital and post-coital pleasure all over again! 'You know—a little like enjoying a delicious slice of gooey chocolate cake and anticipating having another slice but just knowing that it really wouldn't be good for you.'

Lucan gave a humourless smile. 'Interesting euphemism.'

Lexie returned that smile with a bright, meaningless one of her own. 'I thought so.'

'Did you know that chocolate can be addictive?'

'Only in its true form,' Lexie came back pertly.

Lucan's mouth tightened. 'Lexie, we just made love together, and it was really good, so why are we arguing?'

It *had* been really good, Lexie acknowledged heavily. More than good for her. It had been magical—so much more than anything Lexie could ever have imagined. Until she had realised that the reason it had been so magical, so wonderful, was because she was in love with Lucan…

'I told you earlier—we always argue when we bother to talk to each other. This time let's just put it down to the fact that I'm a grouch when I've been ill.' She shrugged.

Lucan studied her for long, tense seconds. Seconds when Lexie's defiant gaze didn't so much as waver from his. 'I don't accept that as an excuse.'

'Newsflash, Lucan—I really don't give a damn what you do or don't accept,' she told him wearily. 'I'm not denying we both had a good time earlier. The point is that we aren't now. That being the case, would you please just accept that I want you to go?'

Lucan eyed her frustratedly, knowing by the defiant way she continued to meet his gaze that they really weren't going to solve anything tonight by continuing their present conversation.

'Okay, I'll go,' he agreed abruptly. 'We'll talk again in the morning.'

'In the morning I'm out of here. With or without you!' she stated firmly.

Lucan's impatience intensified. 'I'm the one with the car, Lexie, and I'm no longer sure I'll be ready to leave in the morning.' He had no intention of going anywhere until he and Lexie had stopped arguing enough to make some sense out of what had just happened.

'Then I'll get a train home.'

'And if there aren't any?'

'There are,' she assured him with satisfaction.

Lucan's eyes narrowed. 'And you know this how…?'

Too late Lexie realised she had once again fallen into the trap of revealing too much. Of saying too much. Of knowing too much. 'I checked on the running of the trains before coming here.' Her chin rose as she told the lie. Visiting her grandmother, as she did regularly, Lexie had been conversant with the running times of the trains to Stourbridge for several years now. 'Just in case I decided to leave,' she added.

Lucan gave a humourless smile as he shook his head. 'You really are something else!'

Lexie was starting to feel ill again. 'Goodnight, Lucan,' she said firmly.

His nostrils flared as he breathed out his frustration. 'I'm really not that easily dismissed!'

Lexie felt a shiver down her spine at the warning she heard in his tone. 'As we aren't likely to meet again after tomorrow, there's really no need for me to know that, is there?'

He shrugged those broad and magnificently bare shoulders. 'As I said, I'm not that easily dismissed.'

'You just were!'

He gave a tight smile. 'Goodnight, Lexie.' He grabbed his jumper from the floor before strolling unhurriedly to the door. 'We will talk again in the morning,' he repeated firmly.

'Maybe I won't be here in the morning.'

Lucan turned at the door. 'Then I'll hunt you down when I get back to London,' he informed her calmly.

Too calmly. And with too much of a sense of purpose for Lexie's comfort… 'The arrogant and elusive Lucan St Claire, chasing after a woman?' she taunted. 'Whatever next?'

His eyes narrowed to glittering onyx slits. 'Believe me, Lexie, if you put me to the trouble of coming after then you won't like what happens next.'

Her eyes widened. 'Are you threatening me?'

'Just stating a fact.'

She gave an impatient sigh. 'Can't we just leave things the way they are?'

His jaw tightened. 'No.'

She grimaced. 'I had a feeling you were going to say that.'

'Then you weren't disappointed, were you?' Lucan drawled unsympathetically. 'Sweet dreams, Lexie,' he added huskily, before closing the door softly behind him.

Lexie's fingernails dug painfully into the palms of her hands where they clenched in the pockets of her robe as painful resistance to the urge she felt to run after him. To ask Lucan to stay. To beg him to hold her and never let her go…

But how ridiculous was it to expect that Lucan, a man who had never wanted to stay with any woman, let alone the granddaughter of Sian Thomas, would ever want to do that?

Almost as ridiculous as Lexie having allowed herself to fall in love with him…

'It's midday, sleepyhead. Time to wake up.'

Lexie kept her eyes firmly closed. She'd guessed from the nearness of Lucan's voice that he was standing beside the bed, where she lay with her face partly buried in the pillows.

She didn't care what time it was. She didn't want Lucan to know she was awake. Didn't want to look at him again. Didn't want to start last night's argument with him all over again.

She hadn't been able to sleep at all after Lucan had left her bedroom the night before—too upset, too emotionally raw to be able to turn off her thoughts and relax into sleep. How could she possibly relax when she had been stupid enough to fall in love with Lucan?

Just thinking about it now was enough to make her feel ill all over again!

Lucan stared down at Lexie frustratedly. He was pretty sure that she was awake and choosing to ignore him. And after the virtually sleepless night he'd had he wasn't in the mood to humour her. Instead he strode over to the window and pulled the curtains back, instantly letting in the bright sunlight.

'Ooh! Ow! That is *so* mean!' Lexie sat up abruptly, her eyes screwed up against the brightness, her hair standing up in tangled tufts. She looked so much like an indignant hedgehog that Lucan had trouble holding back a smile. 'That had better be coffee you have in that mug, otherwise you're a dead man!' she warned him fiercely.

'It's coffee, with milk and two sugars, just the way you like it,' Lucan confirmed mockingly as he strode back to the bedside and handed her the steaming mug of coffee he had brought with him as a peace offering. 'Not a morning person, I see?'

'Don't start on me, Lucan!' She scowled as she pushed some of that dark hair away from her face. 'And according to you it isn't still morning.' She had both hands wrapped about the warmth of the mug as she took a reviving sip.

A *cute* indignant hedgehog, Lucan revised. Even with her hair tangled, her face bare of make-up and little creases in one of her cheeks from where she had been in deep sleep on the pillow, Lexie still managed to arouse him. Damn it!

He crossed his arms in front of his chest. 'Do you want to go to the bathroom first, or shall we finish our conversation now?'

She looked up at him from beneath lowered brows. 'Persistent, aren't you!'

Lucan shrugged. 'I prefer to think of it as single-minded.'

'Hmm...'

'Was that, *Yes, Lucan, I would like to use the bathroom first,* or was it, *Okay, we can talk now...?*'

'Neither.' Lexie shook her head. 'It was please go away until I've woken up properly!'

'That isn't very polite when I've brought you coffee,' Lucan admonished.

She looked more disgruntled than ever. 'How long have you been up?'

'Five hours or so.' He shrugged. 'I managed to get a lot of the work that I brought with me done while you slept the morning away.' Working had also succeeded in keeping Lucan occupied while he waited for Lexie to get up. Until he had finally got tired of waiting and decided to wake her himself.

'That's good.' She nodded unconcernedly. 'I'm really

pleased for you. Now, would you just go away and leave me to enjoy my coffee in peace?'

Lucan had no idea—when this woman irritated him, annoyed him, frustrated him—why it was that she could still manage to make him laugh, too.

'Don't tell me.' Lexie looked up at Lucan wearily as she heard him chuckle. The few hours' sleep she had managed had not been in the least restful when she'd known she still had to face Lucan again this morning. 'People don't talk to you in this disrespectful way.'

'No, they don't.' He still smiled. 'But I could probably get used to it…' he added enigmatically.

Lexie straightened, more unnerved by having Lucan standing beside her bed than she wanted him to realize. Her pulse was racing, every part of her completely aware of how dark and powerful he looked in another black sweater and black denims. 'Luckily for you, you don't have to.'

'No?'

'No—*Damn!*' Lexie swore irritably as, having turned to place her empty mug on the bedside table, she heard something fall onto the carpeted floor. 'What—?'

She froze as she bent over the side of the bed and looked down at exactly what had fallen to the floor.

Everything stopped for Lexie in that moment. Movement. Breathing. Even her heart felt as if it had stopped beating as she stared down at the broken chain and the locket, where they had fallen onto the green carpet.

'Don't!' she protested when Lucan instantly went down on his haunches to retrieve them.

'What the hell *is* it with you and this damned locket?' Lucan rasped. He scooped the locket and chain up in his hand, taking a step back out of Lexie's reach as he straightened. 'Maybe you really *do* keep a photograph of a secret lover in here?' He frowned darkly. 'Maybe I should take a look…'

'*No!*' Even as she protested Lexie desperately threw back the bedclothes and tried to stand up.

Too late.

Far, far too late!

Lucan had already flicked the clasp open and was looking down at the two photographs inside the locket, a perplexed frown darkening his brow.

Long seconds, a minute passed, with no other sound in the room but the two of them breathing. Lexie's was laboured; Lucan barely breathed at all.

Finally he looked up. His face was deathly pale, his cheekbones raw beneath the tautness of his skin. His mouth was a thin, uncompromising line. A pulse pounded in his tightly clenched jaw. And eyes that had been dark and teasing a few minutes ago were now as cold and hard as the onyx they resembled.

Those black eyes narrowed dangerously. 'Who the hell *are* you?'

CHAPTER THIRTEEN

'GIVE me the locket, Lucan,' Lexie demanded shakily as she held out her hand.

Instead of complying, Lucan tightened his fingers instinctively about the piece of jewellery, uncaring of the open clasp digging painfully into his palm. The contents of the locket were firmly branded—seared—into his brain as he took a step away from that questing hand.

There were two photographs inside the locket. One of a grey-haired man, obviously in his sixties, although his face was still handsome as he smiled warmly at the person taking the photograph. A hard and aristocratic face that Lucan had instantly recognised as belonging to his father, Alexander.

The second photograph was of a woman. Only the streaks of grey in her shoulder-length black hair betrayed her age. Her face was youthfully unlined as she, too, laughed happily towards the camera.

It was a beautiful face: creamy brow, wide blue eyes, a pert nose and a wide and smiling mouth. Facial features too reminiscent of the woman now standing in front of Lucan for the two of them not to be related.

'I asked who you are...' Lucan repeated, icily soft.

Lexie swallowed hard, her breathing still shallow, and

she felt slightly light-headed as she looked at the pale and arrogant stranger who now stood before her.

Lucan the lover had gone.

The teasing Lucan had also disappeared. And in his place was a man who exuded such cold and remorseless fury Lexie felt as if she could almost reach out and touch it.

She shook her head. 'I can explain, Lucan—'

'Then I advise you to do it! *Now,*' he added harshly. 'A good place to start would be the name of the woman in the photograph.'

Lexie staggered back from the relentless force of Lucan's anger, sitting down on the edge of the bed before she fell down.

She had only intended working at the St Claire Corporation for three days—satisfying her curiosity about the St Claire family and then just walking away, hopefully with that curiosity satisfied. Since coming to know Lucan she had realised exactly how dangerous it would be for him ever to know she was the granddaughter of Sian Thomas.

As dangerous as Lexie falling in love with Lucan...

Lucan who now looked at her with such dislike, such cold contempt, that it sent an icy shiver down the length of her spine.

'Tell me, damn it!' he ordered savagely.

Lexie moistened lips that had gone dry. 'Her name is Sian Thomas...'

'Louder, Lexie,' Lucan bit out coldly.

Her chin rose. 'Her name is Sian Thomas. She's my grandmother,' she added softly as hot tears burned the backs of her eyes.

Lucan drew in a harshly hissing breath. He had known, of course—had guessed that the woman in the locket could only be one woman. The woman his father had loved. The same woman who had been responsible for the destruction of Lucan's family twenty-five years ago.

Sian Thomas.

Unbelievably, Lexie's grandmother!

He had known that Sian Thomas was a widow when his father had met her all those years ago, and that she'd had a nineteen-year-old daughter. He had just never thought of that daughter as having married and possibly having had children—a daughter of her own.

Lucan turned and strode forcefully over to stand in front of the window with his back to the room. He fought for control, not even attempting to look out onto the grounds but instead opening his hand so that he could once again look down at the locket in the palm of his hand.

Dear God, these photographs of his distinguished grey-haired father and Lexie's gracefully beautiful grandmother could have been of himself and Lexie in thirty years' time. Their similarity to the two was so marked!

'Lucan—'

'Don't say anything for the moment, Lexie,' he warned between gritted teeth.

'Alexandra.'

Lucan turned sharply. 'What?'

Lexie drew in a shaky breath as she saw the hard set of Lucan's face and the hands clenched at his sides. 'My full name is Alexandra Claire Hamilton. I was named for my step-grandfather,' she added unnecessarily.

Those dark eyes narrowed icily. 'As far as I'm aware my father never married your grandmother.'

'No,' she conceded, aware that Lucan had meant the remark to be insulting. 'But my mother still called him Papa Alex, and I called him Grandpa Alex.'

Lucan's nostrils flared sneeringly. 'My father was the Duke of Stourbridge!'

Her breath caught in her throat. 'You're implying *that* was the reason the two of them never married?'

'Why else?' he scorned. 'It would never have done, would it? The illustrious Duke of Stourbridge married to a—'

'Don't you *dare* say anything insulting about my grandmother!' Lexie said emotionally. 'Don't you dare, Lucan!' Her eyes flashed. 'Whether or not he was married to my grandmother, your father *was* my Grandpa Alex.' She raised her chin defiantly.

He nodded. 'And when did you intend sharing that little fact with me?'

Lexie gave a shiver of apprehension as she felt the full blast of Lucan's icy fury. 'I didn't,' she assured him shakily.

'I don't believe you,' he snapped.

She shook her head from side to side. 'I didn't plan any of this, Lucan. I—It just happened.'

Lucan's top lip turned back scornfully. 'You can't really expect me to believe that you had no idea who I was the day you came to work for me?'

'I didn't say that.' Impatience edged her tone. 'Of course I knew who you were. I just—I had no intention of ever telling you of my relationship to—to Sian Thomas…' she added lamely. 'I was curious, okay?' she continued defensively when Lucan just continued to look down his arrogant nose at her—as if she were a particularly unpleasant species of insect that had wandered into his line of vision. 'I didn't even know you existed until I was fourteen, when my mother explained…explained the situation to me.'

'No doubt your mother's version of what happened

twenty-five years ago differs greatly from my own,' Lucan bit out contemptuously.

Lexie stood up abruptly. 'You were only eleven when it happened, Lucan.'

'And you were told at fourteen. Do you seriously think those few extra years—fifteen years after the event—make you any better equipped to know, to comment on what did or didn't happen?' he scorned.

No, of course she didn't. In fact, Lexie had become aware over the past few days of just how sketchy her knowledge was concerning the whys and hows of her grandmother's relationship with Alexander St Claire twenty-five years ago...

She had only been fourteen years old, for goodness' sake, teetering on the brink of womanhood. Her grandmother and Grandpa Alex's love story had seemed so romantic to her. A Greek tragedy with a happy ending.

Except Lexie had realised since coming to Mulberry Hall with Lucan, witnessing firsthand his bitterness, his underlying sadness when he looked at that portrait of his father in the west gallery, that there had been no happy ending for Lucan and the rest of his family...

'Maybe you should talk to my grandmother—'

'Are you *insane*?' Lucan burst out incredulously.

Lexie bristled. 'She's the only one still alive who can tell you what really happened.'

'I was there, Lexie. I know what "really" happened!' he assured coldly.

She shook her head. 'I don't think you do. I *know* my grandmother, Lucan,' she defended as he gave a scathing snort. 'She's not the sort of woman who would ever deliberately hurt anyone.'

'You're predisposed to think that, Lexie.' He looked at

her pityingly. 'You obviously love her, and as such she can do no wrong in your eyes,' he added with hard dismissal.

'You must have loved your father once, and yet you've seemed quite willing to believe the worst of him all these years!' she came back defensively.

Lucan became very still. He *had* loved his father once—had looked up to him, believed him to be omnipotent, a man who could do no wrong. What a complete fallacy that had turned out to be!

'I have no intention of discussing my feelings for my father with you, Lexie,' he grated. 'At this moment I'm far more interested in knowing exactly what you thought you were doing—what you expected, when you went to bed with me,' he said softly.

'What I *expected*…?' she gasped.

'Yes,' Lucan snapped tersely. 'You said earlier that you came to work for me because you were curious. Curious about what, exactly?'

'You. Your family.' Lexie tried to explain. 'I was there the day of Grandpa Alex's funeral. I stood at the back of the church, watching the three of you—Gideon, Jordan and Lucan St Claire—as you sat in the front pew, publicly mourning the man you had privately shunned for twenty-five years.' She gave a shake of her head, her voice hardening. 'While my grandmother—the woman who had loved him and been loved by him for those same twenty-five years—had to sit at home in her cottage and mourn him. For that alone I've always hated you!'

'Me?'

'Yes, you!' She glared accusingly. 'The high and mighty fifteenth Duke of Stourbridge.'

'I have already told you that I don't use the title!' A nerve pulsed in Lucan's tightly clenched jaw.

'I'm sure you used it when you ensured that my

grandmother didn't attend your father's funeral,' Lexie scorned.

He shook his head. 'I have absolutely no idea what you're talking about.'

'Please don't lie to me, Lucan.' She sighed. 'At least let there be truth between us now.'

'Truth?' he repeated incredulously. 'You dare to talk to me of truth when from the moment we first met every word out of your mouth has been a lie?' He gave a disgusted shake of his head. 'God knows how you managed to manoeuvre things with Premier Personnel so that you came to work for me in the first place—'

'My parents own the company.'

'Your—!'

'They're away on a cruise at the moment, and left me in charge,' she said miserably.

Lucan gave a disbelieving shake of his head. 'And poor misguided Jessica gave you exactly the opening you needed!'

Lexie groaned. 'I'll admit what I did was wrong—'

'Because you got caught out? Or because you don't truly believe that this is none of your business?' Lucan was still having trouble believing, accepting that Lexie was the granddaughter of Sian Thomas, of all women. Except he still held the undeniable proof in his hand. And, of course, had Lexie's own confession…

'None of my business?' she repeated quietly, indignantly. 'Tell me, Lucan, did you know that my grandmother still lives in the same cottage in the village that she's owned for the past twenty-five years?'

He frowned darkly. 'In Stourbridge?'

'In Stourbridge,' she confirmed stonily.

'Owned?' he sneered. 'Or was she given it by my father,

so that he could have his mistress close at hand while he continued to live out a lie here, with his wife and sons?'

'You know, Lucan, I would feel sorry for you if you weren't so damned arrogant.' Lexie looked at him pityingly. 'For your information, my grandmother didn't come to live in Stourbridge until *after* your mother and father were divorced.'

Lucan sighed his impatience. 'I don't really see what this has to do with anything—'

'Because you aren't listening!' Lexie gave an exasperated shake of her head. 'Not that it's your business, but my grandmother bought her cottage with money left to her by my real grandfather when he died. But that isn't what's important. Do you have any idea why she still lives in Stourbridge, Lucan? Why she continues to stay on in the village alone? In spite of the gossip that still circulates about her and your father? Despite my parents' repeated entreaties for her to move to London and live with them?'

'No doubt you're about to enlighten me,' Lucan scorned uninterestedly.

'She stays here out of *love*, Lucan,' Lexie told him proudly. 'She can't bear to leave the place where she and Grandpa Alex were so happy together. Where he's buried.' Her voice broke emotionally. 'It's been eight years, Lucan, and yet she still visits his grave several times a week. Can any of your family say the same?'

'We live in London—'

'So do I. But I always go and place fresh flowers on Grandpa Alex's grave whenever I come to visit my grandmother, which is usually every couple of months. We went there together yesterday morning,' she added softly.

Lucan's eyes widened. 'That's why you were gone for over two hours…?'

'Yes,' she sighed.

Lucan eyed her coldly. 'How does your grandmother feel about your being here with me?'

Lexie bit her top lip. 'She was naturally…concerned once she knew that you had no idea who I was.'

'And does who you are have anything to do with your not wanting to go to the Bartons' for dinner yesterday evening? John didn't recognise you, but perhaps Cathy would have done…?'

Lexie nodded. 'I think she may be someone I knew in the village when I was younger.'

He gave a humourless laugh. 'And I was stupid enough to think it was because I had upset you!'

'You *did* upset me—'

'Not enough, obviously!'

Her chin rose stubbornly. 'You might be interested to know that my grandmother talked to Grandpa Alex about you yesterday morning—told him that you were staying at Mulberry Hall. She also told him how successful you are. How proud he would be. Of *all* his sons.'

Lucan mouth twisted derisively. 'I'm sure this is all very touching, Lexie—'

'Don't you dare say anything insulting about the love my grandmother and Grandpa Alex felt for each other!' she warned him heatedly. 'Don't you dare!'

He sighed heavily. 'Okay, Lexie, I won't do that. I'll leave you with your perfect little dream world intact.'

'I'm not naïve, Lucan. I know people were hurt because the two of them fell in love—'

'Hurt?' he echoed coldly. 'My family was destroyed because of it. As for my mother—! It's been twenty-five years, Lexie. Twenty-five years! My mother was only thirty-two at the time, and very beautiful, but she's never remarried. Never even let another man into her life, as far as I'm aware. She's still beautiful, and young enough to have another life with someone else, but because of what *he* did to her—his betrayal of their marriage with your grandmother—'

'You have to *stop*, Lucan!' Lexie choked. 'So much bitterness…! Can't you see how destructive it all is? Hasn't enough damage been done without letting it affect your own life in this way?'

Lucan looked at her coldly. 'You don't think it was bitter and destructive to go to bed with me out of some sort of misguided need for revenge?'

'Revenge?' Lexie repeated, absolutely astounded. Was he insane? 'What sort of revenge could I possibly hope to achieve by going to bed with you?'

'How the hell should I know?' he rasped. 'Perhaps you were hoping that I would fall in love with you, and then you could laugh in my face when I told you how I felt…?'

Lexie did laugh—but not in Lucan's face. She laughed out of self-derision; she was the one who had fallen in love with Lucan, not the other way round! 'Five minutes in your company—a minute!—would be enough to tell any woman that you don't know the meaning of the word love, let alone how to feel the emotion!'

'Really?' Lucan became very still, deathly calm again—the sort of cold, remorseless calm that anyone with any sense of self-preservation would know to back away from.

Lexie might have behaved recklessly by going anywhere near Lucan, might have committed the ultimate in stupidity by falling in love with him, but she wasn't totally bereft of a sense of self-preservation. 'I think it's time I left, Lucan.'

'To go back to London?'

She shook her head. 'To my grandmother's cottage. I need to see her before I leave—assure her that all is well.' Even if it wasn't! 'I'll get a train back to London later today.'

'Being completely conversant with the train times, as you said.'

'Yes.'

Lucan nodded abruptly. 'I trust you'll forgive me if I don't stand on the platform and wave you a fond farewell…?'

Did hearts really break? Until that moment Lexie hadn't thought that they did. But if they didn't, then what was the wrenching pain in her chest just at the thought of never seeing Lucan again after today? Of knowing that he was somewhere in the world, hating her…?

She gave a shaky smile. 'I'll forgive you, Lucan.'

'I won't forgive *you*,' he came back gratingly.

Yes, hearts really did break, Lexie accepted desolately. In fact they shattered. 'Goodbye, Lucan.'

He stared at her with those cold, analytical eyes for several long seconds more, before turning on his heel and striding purposefully from the bedroom.

Lexie moved to once again sit down shakily on the side of the bed, burying her face in her hands as she at last let hot, scalding tears cascade down her cheeks.

It wasn't until much later—after Lexie had visited her grandmother and was sitting on the train taking her back to London—that she realised Lucan hadn't returned her locket and chain to her…

CHAPTER FOURTEEN

'LEXIE, I know it's late, but there's someone here to see you...'

'It's okay—Brenda, isn't it? I told you I can see myself in,' drawled a familiar—achingly familiar—voice, before Lexie had a chance to look up from the paperwork on her desk, which she had been trying to finish before leaving work for the evening.

But her head snapped up now, the colour draining from her face as she saw Lucan looming tall and dark behind Brenda where she stood protectively in the doorway. Devastatingly handsome Lucan, dressed in one of those dark tailored suits he favoured, with a snowy-white shirt beneath and a black wool overcoat that reached almost down to his ankles.

It had been five days since the two of them parted so ig-nominiously in Gloucestershire. Five long and painful days when Lexie had see-sawed between aching to see Lucan again and the certainty that seeing him would only make the heartache she was suffering even harder to bear.

Her gaze quickly returned to his face, searching those austerely handsome features for some sign of why Lucan was here now. That sculpted mouth was unsmiling, and those dark eyes returned her gaze unblinkingly, almost challengingly...

Lexie's eyes veered away from those penetrating depths and she smiled at her assistant instead. 'You get along home, Brenda,' she encouraged the other woman as she slowly stood up. 'Mr St Claire is probably here to discuss his account.' Although Lexie very much doubted that 'account' really described the invoice she had sent to the St Claire Corporation two days ago, on behalf of Premier Personnel.

She moved to stand in front of her desk once Brenda had left, after shooting her a sympathetic grimace, relieved that she looked businesslike today, in a black suit with a pale blue blouse beneath the jacket, her hair pulled back from her face and secured with a black clasp at her crown.

'Do you have a query on your account, Mr St Claire?' she prompted lightly.

Lucan strolled farther into the office. Lexie's nervousness increased as he softly closed the door behind him before turning slowly, his expression still totally unreadable. 'Unless I'm mistaken, the invoice submitted from Premier Personnel was for zero?'

Lexie leant back against her desk. 'That's correct.'

Even *thinking* of sending Lucan a bill for the two days she had supposedly worked for him had smacked of demanding payment for services rendered; Lexie felt bad enough already, without that. She certainly hadn't expected that the invoice would bring Lucan here in person. Had she…?

'Was there something else, Mr St Claire?'

Lucan walked towards her, once again reminding Lexie of that jungle cat stalking its prey. His steps were measured and somehow menacing, his dark and predatory gaze holding her captive. 'Why no charge, Lexie? You did work for me for two days, after all.'

'Not really.' She shook her head, her hands moving to

rest on the desk either side of her. She gripped the edge tightly, so that Lucan shouldn't see how badly her hands were shaking just at being near him again. 'I—I just thought it best.'

'For whom?'

'For all concerned.' Lexie grimaced.

'Hmm.' Lucan nodded slowly. 'Would you like to go out to dinner?'

Lexie's head snapped back as she eyed him warily. 'Go out to dinner…?' She moistened her lips nervously.

He gave a humourless smile. 'Let's not start repeating each other's words again, hmm?'

Lexie was too stunned by the invitation to be able to think of any coherent words of her own. It was traumatic enough that Lucan was here at all, without the complete shock of having him invite her to dinner. She swallowed hard. 'I'm not sure I understand.'

Lucan had known by Lexie's shocked expression when she first saw him, and the wariness in her eyes now, that his dinner invitation was the last thing she had been expecting. After the way they had parted five days ago, and his response to discovering she was Sian Thomas's granddaughter, it was probably a natural reaction.

Lexie looked very professional today, in a black suit, with the wild ebony of her hair pulled back from the paleness of her face. Very un-Lexie-like!

'I believe there are still some things the two of us need to discuss,' he bit out grimly.

Lexie watched him guardedly as he stood only inches away from her. 'And I thought we had agreed to disagree on the subject of my grandmother and your father?'

Lucan thrust his hands into the pockets of his overcoat to stop himself from giving in to the impulse he felt to remove the clip from Lexie's hair and so allow it to cascade wildly about her shoulders as it usually did. His fingers instead came into contact with the rectangular box at the bottom of the right-hand pocket. He removed the velvet-covered box, glancing down at it before holding it out to Lexie.

'You forgot this when you left…'

Her expression became even more wary, and she eyed the box as if it were a snake about to strike her a lethal blow.

'It's only your locket, Lexie,' Lucan drawled.

'Oh,' she breathed softly, and was very careful that her fingers shouldn't come into contact with his hand as she took the box from him to flip up the lid and look inside. 'You've had it repaired…' She looked up at him almost accusingly.

Lucan's mouth tightened. 'There seemed little point in not doing so once I knew of its contents.'

Little point at all, Lexie accepted as she gently ran a finger over the surface of her locket. The gold chain looped through it was now intact.

'Unless there was some other reason you didn't want me to have it repaired…?'

Her gaze flicked back up at Lucan. She was very aware of his close proximity. Of the tangy smell of his aftershave. The warmth of his body…

'I—No—no other reason,' she assured him huskily.

He nodded abruptly. 'According to my mother, the locket and necklace once belonged to my father's grandmother—a lady he was very fond of.'

Lexie bristled. 'If you're trying to say this is some sort of family heirloom and you want it returned—'

'I'm not,' Lucan dismissed impatiently. 'Why do you always assume the worst of me, Lexie?'

Lexie chose not to answer that particular question in

favour of asking a more pressing—shocking—one. 'You've shown my locket to your *mother*?'

He gave another inclination of his head. 'She believes my father must have loved you very much to have given you something that meant so much to him.'

Lexie had absolutely no doubt as to how much her Grandpa Alex had loved her. How much he had loved *all* his beloved Sian's family. 'You showed my locket to your mother?' she said again, incredulously.

Lucan gave a rueful smile. 'You're starting to repeat yourself now, Lexie. Or would you prefer I call you Alexandra?' He quirked dark brows.

'No, I would *not* prefer that you call me Alexandra!' she snapped, and moved determinedly away from the sensuous lethargy, the heated reaction Lucan's closeness was starting to have on her senses after she had felt cold for so long.

'Because it's what your family call you?'

Lexie dropped the closed velvet jewellery box into her handbag behind the desk before straightening to answer him suspiciously. 'How do you know what my family call me?'

Lucan shrugged. 'That's one of the things I would like to discuss with you over dinner.'

Lexie moved her head from side to side. 'I don't want to have dinner.'

'With me? Or at all?'

'At all!' She'd had absolutely no appetite since returning from Gloucestershire five days ago. In fact, the mere thought of food made her feel ill—to a degree that she had lost several pounds in weight over the past few days! 'I can't believe you took my necklace and showed it to your mother!' she muttered again.

'You seem a bit hung up on that fact.'

'Of course I'm "hung up" on it!' Lexie snapped. 'You

had no right to do that, Lucan,' she told him emotionally. 'No right at all.'

He gave a rueful grimace. 'Lexie, I took your advice after you left Mulberry Hall five days ago.'

'*My* advice?' she repeated incredulously. 'I'm pretty sure I didn't say anything that day about taking my locket and showing it to your mother!' All Lexie remembered about that day was her complete devastation at the realisation that she had fallen in love with this man.

Seeing Lucan again, being near him again, only served to show her how deeply she loved him. How much she wished that things could be different between them. That the two of them were free to have a relationship, even if it only lasted a matter of days or weeks.

Instead, Lexie had fallen in love with the one man who would never love her…

'No,' Lucan conceded dryly. 'But you did suggest that I talk to your grandmother,' he added softly.

Lexie's eyes widened as she stared across the desk at him. 'I— You—'

'I think perhaps you should sit down, Lexie—before you fall down!' Lucan drawled derisively.

Yes, she should perhaps sit down. No, not perhaps—she *had* to sit down, Lexie acknowledged as her legs began to tremble. She dropped weakly down into the chair behind the desk.

'You've spoken to my grandmother…?'

'At length,' Lucan confirmed softly. 'Want to change your mind about coming out to dinner with me…?' He lifted a mocking brow.

'This was a much better idea than going out and eating dinner in a restaurant,' Lucan approved huskily an hour or so later, as he and Lexie sat opposite each other at the breakfast bar in the kitchen of her apartment.

Their conversation had been put on hold while Lucan drove them there from the offices of Premier Personnel, stopping briefly to buy a selection of cheeses and fruits from a local delicatessen, along with a bottle of red wine, which Lucan had acquired from the off-licence next door.

In fact, the whole scenario of sitting in the kitchen, food spread out before them on the breakfast bar, reminded Lucan strongly of their last evening together at Mulberry Hall, when he and Lexie had eaten cheese and biscuits together before making love…

Especially so as Lexie looked more like herself now. She had disappeared to her bedroom as soon as they'd arrived, emerging ten minutes later having changed into a fitted cream woollen jumper and figure-hugging denims, and with her hair released in disarray about her shoulders.

She grimaced now. 'I'm sure you're no more eager than I am to make a scene in public.'

'A scene?' he repeated slowly. 'I'm hoping it won't come to that!'

'No doubt that's a case of hope springing eternal!' She took a sip of the red wine.

'Possibly,' Lucan allowed dryly. 'You need to eat something, Lexie, You're looking very pale.'

Her eyes flashed deeply blue as she glared across the breakfast bar at him. 'We've been very busy at the office.'

He frowned. 'I wasn't implying anything else…'

Lexie drew in a ragged breath, knowing she had over-reacted to a perfectly innocent observation; she *was* very pale, and she *did* need to eat. Except, more than ever, she had a feeling that food would choke her!

It wasn't helping her already frayed nerves that Lucan had taken off his overcoat and jacket while she was in her bedroom changing out of her work clothes. His tie had also been removed, and the top button of his shirt undone, revealing a tantalising glimpse of the dark hair on his muscle-rippling chest…

'Sorry.' Lexie gave another grimace. 'Things have just been a bit hectic the past few days, with both my parents away.' Despite her self-assurances to the contrary, when she had disappeared out of the office the previous week… 'I suppose that at least shows me you haven't felt compelled to damage the reputation of Premier Personnel after last week…' she added lamely.

Lucan's brows lowered over narrowed dark eyes. 'What happened between us is personal, Lexie, not business-related.'

'It's—good of you to say so.'

'But unexpected?' he guessed dryly.

'Maybe,' she answered guardedly.

'It really pains you to have to admit that I'm capable of doing anything decent, doesn't it?'

'Not at all,' Lexie protested. 'You have every right to want to make trouble for Premier Personnel after the way I behaved.'

Lucan regarded her quizzically. 'I seem to remember that you said Premier Personnel belongs to your parents, and I have absolutely no reason to wish them harm.'

Just her, Lexie accepted heavily.

She had behaved badly the previous week. Worse than badly. She had been totally stupid in going anywhere near the St Claire family. All Lexie had done was rake up a past that would have been better left alone.

'Thank you,' she said softly.

Lucan leant back on his bar chair to look across at her.

'You know, Lexie, I'm not sure I know what to do with all this self-flagellation!' He gave a rueful shake of his head. 'Where's the woman who told me she doesn't give a damn about anything I do or say? The woman who felt no hesitation in telling me exactly what she thought of me?'

Lexie gave a humourless smile. 'She grew up.'

'Pity,' he drawled.

Her eyes widened. 'You would rather I went back to being rude and outspoken?'

'Hell, yes,' Lucan assured her unhesitatingly. 'At least then I'd have an excuse to kiss you into silence.'

Lexie stared across at him, her lips frozen on a silent *oh* of surprise. Shock, actually. Was Lucan saying he *wanted* an excuse to kiss her…?

Her mouth had gone as dry as her lips felt. 'Do you need an excuse?'

'Not really,' he drawled. 'But it might be handy to use in my defence when you turn on me like a wildcat afterwards!'

Lexie gave a slow shake of her head. 'I don't understand…'

Lucan grimaced, knowing he had a lot of things he needed to tell Lexie before they could even begin to talk about a relationship—the possibility of a relationship—between the two of them. He was here now because he owed Lexie the truth. He had no reason to believe that Lexie would want anything else from him once he had given her that.

'No, I don't suppose you do.' He sighed, taking a sip of his own wine before continuing. 'From what I said to you earlier, you will have gathered that I've seen and talked with both your grandmother and my mother since we last spoke together.'

'Yes.' Lexie still eyed him warily.

Lucan nodded. 'What I haven't explained is that they have also seen and spoken to each other.'

She gasped. 'Nanna Sian and your mother?' Her hand shook slightly as she carefully replaced her wine glass on the breakfast bar.

Lucan smiled. 'My mother flew from Edinburgh to Gloucestershire with me yesterday.'

'In the family-owned helicopter?' she guessed.

'As it happens, yes.'

'Which you flew?'

'Again, yes... Is there a problem with that?' He frowned.

'Not at all,' Lexie assured him wryly; it only served as a reminder of the social and financial differences between the two of them, as well as the emotional ones. 'So, your mother is in Gloucestershire talking to my Nanna Sian now,' she said pointedly, still totally stunned at the idea of such a thing happening.

'*With* your Nanna Sian, not *to* her,' Lucan corrected.

'But why?' Lexie stood up again restlessly. 'What can the two of them possibly have to talk about after all these years?'

He shrugged. 'I only brought them together, Lexie. I think it's for the two of them to work out what they want to talk about.'

'But why would you do such a thing?' She groaned disbelievingly. 'You all *hate* my poor Nanna!' Her eyes flashed as she became angry. 'If your mother says or does one single thing to hurt her—'

'That's better,' Lucan said with satisfaction. He also stood up, instantly dwarfing Lexie's kitchen—and her. 'What else can I do or say that's going to anger or annoy you?'

'I'm already angry enough—*oof!*' Lexie's breath left

her in a whoosh as Lucan pulled her into his arms and her chest came into hard contact with his. 'Lucan, you—'

Any further protest was cut off as his head lowered and his mouth claimed hers.

Fiercely.

Hungrily.

Lucan continued to hold her, to kiss her, until Lexie stopped being so stunned, and then her arms moved slowly about his waist and she began to return those kisses with a hunger of her own. Deep, searing kisses that plundered the very heart of her.

Finally Lucan pulled back slightly to rest his forehead against hers. 'It isn't my intention, or my mother's, to hurt your Nanna Sian, Lexie,' he assured her gruffly. 'What I did—what I'm trying to do—is put things right after all these years. Sort the situation out enough so that some of the hurt, at least, goes away.'

'But why…?' she asked in a hushed voice.

Good question, Lucan acknowledged self-derisively. And not one that he felt he could answer just yet…

He reached up to grasp Lexie's arms and put her firmly away from him. 'We still have a few things of our own to sort out, Lexie. Firstly, I did not, as you seem to think, stop your grandmother from attending my father's funeral.'

'But—'

'It was your grandmother's decision, Lexie. Not mine. Made, she assures me, because she didn't want to cause any more hurt to my mother and the rest of Alexander's family.'

'But your mother wasn't at the funeral—'

'No, she wasn't. But your grandmother didn't know that,' he pointed out gently. 'It was also because she felt there had already been enough hurt caused because she and

Alexander loved each other that she consistently refused to marry my father when he asked her.'

'What?'

'It's true, Lexie,' he assured her softly. 'If you don't believe me, once we've finished talking you can telephone your grandmother and I'm sure she will confirm everything I'm going to say—okay?'

Lexie was starting to feel as if she were standing on a surface that kept moving beneath her feet. As if every preconceived idea she had ever had was being slowly, determinedly stripped away.

Could any of what Lucan was saying be true? He insisted that it was, knowing that Lexie could indeed telephone her grandmother at any time during this conversation...

'Okay.' Lexie nodded abruptly.

'Let's sit down and drink some more of our wine, Lexie,' Lucan suggested huskily as he pulled back the bar stool for her. 'I still have quite a bit more to say, and we might as well be comfortable,' he added when she paused uncertainly.

Her mouth felt slightly swollen from the force of Lucan's kisses, and her head was buzzing with the things he had already told her. 'Fine.' She sat back on the stool and watched him warily as he moved around the breakfast bar to sit opposite her. 'My grandmother refused to marry your father...?'

Lucan smiled slightly. 'Many, many times.'

'She told you that...?'

'Yes.'

'And you believe her?'

'Yes.'

Lexie picked up her wine glass and took a sip before speaking again. 'I'm more confused than ever...'

'Why she refused? Or why I believe her?' Lucan prompted.

'Both!'

His smile widened. 'Yep, she's still in there!'

She gave him a confused glance. 'Who's still in where?'

Lucan gave a slow shake of his head. 'We haven't got to that part of our conversation yet.'

Lexie scowled at him. 'You can be incredibly annoying at times, Lucan!'

'True,' he accepted with an unapologetic grin. 'Your grandmother told me a lot of other things that I never knew.' He sat forward. 'For instance, did you know that she and my father had known each other for years, loved each other for years, before he even met my mother?'

'That can't be true.' Lexie slowly shook her head. 'Nanna Sian had been married and was widowed. She had a daughter—my mother…'

'The two of them knew each other before Sian married your natural grandfather, Lexie.'

Her eyes were wide. 'I—But how?'

Lucan grimaced. 'They grew up together on the Mulberry Hall estate. Alexander was the son and heir, your grandmother was the daughter of the cook. Needless to say, my own grandfather, the then Duke of Stourbridge, did not look favourably upon the relationship. To such a degree that he set about deliberately separating the two of them,' he added grimly.

Lexie had a terrible feeling she knew exactly where this was going…

'Alexander duly went off to university at Oxford, and within days of his leaving his father had the cook and her daughter relocated to a friend's estate in Norfolk,' Lucan continued darkly. 'Sian and Alexander had agreed that he would write to her as soon as he had a mailing address, and that the two of them would continue to write to each other until he came home at Christmas, when they would try once again to persuade his father into seeing how much in love they were.' Lucan gave a disgusted shake of his head. 'I believe you can guess what happened next?'

Lexie gave a pained frown. 'Alexander's letters to Sian were intercepted by the Duke as soon as they arrived at Mulberry Hall?'

A nerve pulsed in Lucan's clenched jaw. 'Intercepted and destroyed, rather than sent on to where Sian lived in Norfolk,' he confirmed harshly. 'As Sian's letters to Alexander, also care of Mulberry Hall, were duly intercepted and destroyed.'

'Resulting in Sian believing that Alexander had forgotten about her as soon as he was away at university,' Lexie realised heavily.

'Unbelievable, isn't it?' Lucan stood up again restlessly, his expression grim.

Lexie shook her head. 'We didn't have the same technology fifty years ago that we have today. No mobile phones. No email. Sian and Alexander's only means of communication were those letters.'

Lucan nodded tersely. 'Which neither of them received because of my grandfather's intervention. When Alexander came home for the Christmas holidays his father told him that the cook and her daughter had simply handed in their notice and left. That he had no idea where they had gone. That Alexander should just accept that as far as Sian was concerned the relationship was obviously over, and he should just forget about her and get on with his life.'

'It's all so unbelievable it can only be true!' Lexie said achingly.

'Yes.' Lucan drew in a harsh breath. 'Sian eventually married a local boy in Norfolk and had your mother, and my father finished university just in time to take over the running of the estate when his father died suddenly of a heart attack. Knowing what I do now, I'm not sure the old guy even had a heart to *be* attacked!' he added disgustedly as he began to restlessly pace the small confines of the kitchen.

'What he did was wicked and cruel.' Lexie nodded. 'But perhaps he thought he was acting for the best—'

'Your grandmother made the same excuse for him,' Lucan cut in wearily. 'When in reality it *was* just wicked and cruel, as well as totally dishonest,' he insisted firmly. 'But for his interference my father and Sian would have married each other—could have been together for years before they eventually were!'

'And then neither you, nor your two brothers, nor I, would ever have been born.'

The things Lucan had told her—even more of a Greek tragedy than Lexie could have imagined—were incredible. Incredible and so very sad. But, loving Lucan as she did, it was impossible for Lexie to imagine—selfishly—a world without the two of them in it…

'My grandfather deliberately ruined two young people's lives with his machinations.' He gave a disgusted shake of his head. 'Your grandmother has assured me that she was happy with your grandfather, and that she loved him. Not in the way she loved Alexander, but nevertheless she did love him. My father, on the other hand, threw all his energies into running the estate. He only married at all in the end because he needed to provide an heir for that estate. He was almost thirty and my mother only nineteen when they met and married each other. I've spoken to my mother about this, and she assures me it was always a fragile relationship at best—and one that was completely blown apart the moment my father saw Sian again at a weekend house party given by a mutual friend they hadn't even known they had.'

'They never had an affair, Lucan,' Lexie insisted firmly. 'Admittedly, the two of them realising they were still in love with each other all those years later was wrong, so very wrong, when Alexander was married. But I know that they weren't together again until after your father and mother were divorced.'

'I know that, too.'

She raised dark brows. 'Again from my grandmother?'

'Yes.'

She smiled. 'I'm sure you must have been something of a surprise to her! You look so much like Grandpa Alex,' she explained huskily when Lucan looked at her questioningly.

He nodded, his gaze suddenly darkly intense. 'Just as you look like your grandmother...'

Lexie felt the colour warm her cheeks. 'Strange, isn't it?'

'Not strange at all.' Lucan gave a slow shake of his head.

Lexie lowered her gaze, not sure what to say or do next now that Lucan had told her all these things. 'I still don't understand why, Lucan...'

'Why what?'

She frowned. 'Why you went to the trouble of speaking to my grandmother and your mother...'

Lucan looked at her quizzically. 'Do you believe in fate, Lexie?'

'In what context?' she prompted warily.

He gave a rueful smile. 'In the context that almost fifty

years after Alexander fell in love with Sian, against all the odds, against his better judgement, his eldest son has met and fallen in love with Sian's granddaughter...!'

CHAPTER FIFTEEN

LUCAN had no idea what he had expected—hoped—Lexie's reaction would be to his declaration of being in love with her.

Her complete and utter silence certainly wasn't it!

She stared up at him with those huge blue eyes, her expression one of shock more than anything else.

Lucan thrust his hands into his trouser pockets. 'Don't look so worried, Lexie,' he said wryly. 'I'm not expecting some grand announcement of your having fallen in love with me, too. I just… Because of my parents' divorce I didn't want to even believe in love—was determined never to feel the emotion for any woman. And then I met you.' His expression softened. 'From that very first morning I knew you were different.'

'You didn't like me…'

'Oh, I liked you,' he assured her huskily. 'I spent most of that morning imagining making love with you. On the desk. On the floor. Up against the wall.' He gave a shake of his head. 'It was totally out of character! And I was so damned jealous of the easy way you and Andrew Proctor laughed and joked together!' he recalled grimly.

'Really?' Lexie breathed softly.

'Oh, yes,' Lucan confirmed self-derisively. 'Gideon found it most amusing, watching me squirm!'

'Your brother *knew* you felt that way?'

'He guessed, yes. You challenged me, Lexie—drew me to you in a way I had never known before.' He grimaced. 'I knew, feeling that intensity of desire for you, that taking you to Mulberry Hall with me was a bad idea. I just couldn't seem to help myself. Being alone there with you was torturous. But at the same time I felt alive, experienced more emotions than I had ever allowed myself to feel before.'

'And you don't hate your father any more?'

'I'm not sure I ever hated him.' He sighed. 'I was disappointed in him. Felt hurt that he had left us. But, damn it, if he loved his Sian as much as I love you, then I can only feel sorry for the pain and misery he must have felt when he lost her! The joy he must have known when he found her again and they both realised what had happened in the past, that they still loved each other!' he added huskily. 'You asked why I had spoken to your grandmother, been to see my mother, why the two of them are at Mulberry Hall at this very moment coming to some sort of truce?'

Lexie swallowed hard before moistening stiff, barely moving lips. 'And why are they…?'

Lucan's smile was self-derisive. 'Because I didn't want there to be any barriers standing between the two of us while I attempt to persuade you into falling in love with me. Because I want to marry you. To that end, I'm going to haunt you, Lexie,' he told her intensely. 'I'm going to make sure there's no room for any misunderstandings between the two of us. Going to make such a nuisance of myself that you won't be able to turn around and not find me there!'

Lexie could never imagine Lucan's love being a nuisance to *any* woman. Certainly never to her!

Lucan loved her.

Lucan wanted to marry her.

'I don't— You—' Now she sounded like a gibbering

idiot. Probably because she felt like a gibbering idiot! Her heart had felt as if it were breaking these past five days, and now Lucan was offering her paradise.

Lucan's expression was concerned as he reached out and took both her hands in his. 'I *do* love you, Lexie. To distraction. But I don't want that to scare you—'

'I'm not scared, Lucan.' Her fingers tightened about his. 'I'm stunned. In awe. But I'm not scared,' she assured him emotionally.

'In awe?' he repeated uncertainly.

It was an uncertainty that Lexie couldn't bear a moment longer; the Lucan she loved was arrogant, self-assured, never uncertain!

'I already love you, Lucan,' she told him joyfully. 'I fell in love with you while we were at Mulberry Hall, too. Against all the odds. Against my better judgement.' She deliberately quoted his own words back at him. 'I *love* you, Lucan!' She glowed up at him.

Lucan felt as if he'd had all the breath knocked out of his lungs. As if he couldn't form a coherent thought in his head. All he could do was stare at Lexie in wonder. In total, absolute wonder that this beautiful woman, the woman he loved and adored, had just said that she loved him, too.

She smiled up at him teasingly. 'I never thought I would see the day!'

'What day?' Lucan managed to breathe shakily.

'When I would succeed in rendering the arrogantly self-assured Lucan St Claire speechless!' she came back cheekily. 'Tell me—is this going to happen every time I tell you I love you?'

She was back. The outspoken little minx that Lucan had fallen head over heels in love with was most definitely back!

'No,' he growled huskily as he took her firmly in his

arms. '*This* is what's going to happen every time you tell me you love me!'

He lowered his head and his mouth captured hers as he proceeded to show Lexie exactly how much he loved her. How much he would *always* love her.

One month later

'Why are you smiling in that cat-that-got-the-cream way?' Lexie prompted Lucan suspiciously as he chuckled softly.

It was their wedding day. A day when both of their families had gathered together at Mulberry Hall to celebrate their love for each other. A day Lexie had been longing for since the moment Lucan had told her he loved her as much as she loved him.

Lucan grinned down at her as the two of them danced together at their wedding reception in the ballroom at Mulberry Hall. He was so much more relaxed now than the cold and unemotional man Lexie had met five weeks ago. The love he felt for her shone unabashedly in the dark glow of his eyes.

He shook his head. 'Gideon has been secretly laughing at me for the last five weeks because of how much I love you, and I was just savouring the moment—because, looking at his face, I believe he has just learned the joke's now on him!'

Lexie glanced across to where her new brother-in-law stood in the corner of the room, glowering accusingly at Lucan. 'What have you done, Lucan?' She looked up at her husband reprovingly.

'Never mind what I've done.' Lucan tapped her playfully on the nose. 'Just concentrate on what the two of us are going to be doing later.' He grinned down at her wolfishly.

Lexie felt herself melt inside at the heat of desire she could clearly see glowing in his eyes. 'You've become a very wicked man, Lucan St Claire,' she murmured indulgently.

'My Duchess has had a very bad influence on me,' he came back throatily.

His Duchess.

Lexie was now, incredibly, the Duchess of Stourbridge.

But most important of all, she was the woman Lucan loved to distraction.

And he was the man Lexie loved with all her heart.

It was a deep love for each other that she had absolutely no doubt would endure and last for a lifetime.

0211/01a

A STORMY SPANISH SUMMER
by Penny Jordan

Duque Vidal y Salvadores hated Fliss Clairemont—but now he must help her claim her inheritance! As their attraction takes hold, can Vidal admit how wrong he's been about her…?

NOT A MARRYING MAN
by Miranda Lee

Billionaire Warwick Kincaid asked Amber Roberts to move in, but then became distant. Is her time up? The chemistry between them remains *white-hot* and Amber finds it hard to believe that her time with Warwick is *really* over…

SECRETS OF THE OASIS
by Abby Green

After giving herself to Sheikh Salman years ago, Jamilah Moreau's wedding fantasies were crushed. Then Salman spirits her off to a desert oasis and Jamilah discovers he still wants her!

THE HEIR FROM NOWHERE
by Trish Morey

Dominic Pirelli's world falls apart with the news that an IVF mix-up means a stranger is carrying his baby! Dominic is determined to keep waif-like Angelina Cameron close, but who will have custody of the Pirelli heir?

On sale from 18th February 2011
Don't miss out!

Available at WHSmith, Tesco, ASDA, Eason
and all good bookshops
www.millsandboon.co.uk

MODERN

TAMING THE LAST ST CLAIRE
by Carole Mortimer

Gideon St Claire's life revolves around work, so fun-loving Joey McKinley is the sort of woman he normally avoids! Then an old enemy starts looking for revenge and Gideon's forced to protect Joey—day *and* night…

THE FAR SIDE OF PARADISE
by Robyn Donald

A disastrous engagement left Taryn wary of men, but Cade Peredur stirs feelings she's never known before. However, when Cade's true identity is revealed, will Taryn's paradise fantasy dissolve?

THE PROUD WIFE
by Kate Walker

Marina D'Inzeo is finally ready to divorce her estranged husband Pietro—even a summons to join him in Sicily won't deter her! However, with his wife standing before him, Pietro wonders why he ever let her go!

ONE DESERT NIGHT
by Maggie Cox

Returning to the desert plains of Kabuyadir to sell its famous *Heart of Courage* jewel, Gina Collins is horrified the new sheikh is the man who gave her one earth-shattering night years ago.

On sale from 4th March 2011
Don't miss out!

Available at WHSmith, Tesco, ASDA, Eason and all good bookshops
www.millsandboon.co.uk

0211/06

Her Not-So-Secret Diary
by Anne Oliver
Sophie's fantasies stayed secret—until her saucy dream was accidentally e-mailed to her sexy boss! But as their steamy nights reach boiling point, Sophie knows she's in a whole heap of trouble...

The Wedding Date
by Ally Blake
Under no circumstances should Hannah's gorgeous boss, Bradley, be considered her wedding date! Now, if only her disobedient legs would do the *sensible* thing and walk away...

Molly Cooper's Dream Date
by Barbara Hannay
House-swapping with London-based Patrick has given Molly the chance to find a perfect English gentleman! Yet she's increasingly curious about Patrick himself—is the Englishman she wants on the other side of the world?

If the Red Slipper Fits...
by Shirley Jump
It's not *unknown* for Caleb Lewis to find a sexy stiletto in his convertible, but Caleb usually has some recollection of how it got there! He's intrigued to meet the woman it belongs to...

On sale from 4th March 2011
Don't miss out!

Available at WHSmith, Tesco, ASDA, Eason and all good bookshops

www.millsandboon.co.uk

9/MB332

One night with a hot-blooded male!

18th February 2011

18th March 2011

15th April 2011

20th May 2011

www.millsandboon.co.uk

THE Royal
HOUSE OF NIROLI

*The richest royal family in the world—united by blood
and passion, torn apart by deceit and desire*

The Royal House of Niroli: Scandalous Seductions
Penny Jordan & Melanie Milburne
Available 17th December 2010

The Royal House of Niroli: Billion Dollar Bargains
Carol Marinelli & Natasha Oakley
Available 21st January 2011

The Royal House of Niroli: Innocent Mistresses
Susan Stephens & Robyn Donald
Available 18th February 2011

The Royal House of Niroli: Secret Heirs
Raye Morgan & Penny Jordan
Available 18th March 2011

Collect all four!

M&B™

www.millsandboon.co.uk

M&B/RTL3

Discover Pure Reading Pleasure with

**Visit the Mills & Boon website for all
the latest in romance**

🌹 **Buy** all the latest releases, backlist and eBooks

🌹 **Find out** more about our authors and their books

🌹 **Join** our community and chat to authors and other readers

🌹 **Free** online reads from your favourite authors

🌹 **Win** with our fantastic online competitions

🌹 **Sign** up for our free monthly eNewsletter

🌹 **Tell us** what you think by signing up to our reader panel

🌹 **Rate** and review books with our star system

www.millsandboon.co.uk

Follow us at twitter.com/millsandboonuk

Become a fan at facebook.com/romancehq

2 FREE BOOKS
AND A SURPRISE GIFT

We would like to take this opportunity to thank you for reading this Mills & Boon® book by offering you the chance to take TWO more specially selected books from the Modern™ series absolutely FREE! We're also making this offer to introduce you to the benefits of the Mills & Boon® Book Club™—

- **FREE home delivery**
- **FREE gifts and competitions**
- **FREE monthly Newsletter**
- **Exclusive Mills & Boon Book Club offers**
- **Books available before they're in the shops**

Accepting these FREE books and gift places you under no obligation to buy, you may cancel at any time, even after receiving your free books. Simply complete your details below and return the entire page to the address below. You don't even need a stamp!

YES Please send me 2 free Modern books and a surprise gift. I understand that unless you hear from me, I will receive 4 superb new books every month for just £3.30 each, postage and packing free. I am under no obligation to purchase any books and may cancel my subscription at any time. The free books and gift will be mine to keep in any case.

Ms/Mrs/Miss/Mr _____ Initials _____

Surname _____

Address _____

_____ Postcode _____

E-mail _____

Send this whole page to: Mills & Boon Book Club, Free Book Offer, FREEPOST NAT 10298, Richmond, TW9 1BR

Offer valid in UK only and is not available to current Mills & Boon Book Club subscribers to this series. Overseas and Eire please write for details.. We reserve the right to refuse an application and applicants must be aged 18 years or over. Only one application per household. Terms and prices subject to change without notice. Offer expires 30th April 2011. As a result of this application, you may receive offers from Harlequin Mills & Boon and other carefully selected companies. If you would prefer not to share in this opportunity please write to The Data Manager, PO Box 676, Richmond, TW9 1WU.

Mills & Boon® is a registered trademark owned by Harlequin Mills & Boon Limited.
Modern™ is being used as a trademark. The Mills & Boon® Book Club™ is being used as a trademark.